SPORTS
STORIES

KINGFISHER
An imprint of Kingfisher Publications Plc
New Penderel House, 283-288 High Holborn
London WC1V 7HZ

First published by Kingfisher 2000
2 4 6 8 10 9 7 5 3 1 (hardback)
2 4 6 8 10 9 7 5 3 1 (paperback)
1TR/0600/THOM/(FR)/WF100

A CIP catalogue record for this book
is available from the British Library.

ISBN 0 7534 0335 8 (hardback)
ISBN 0 7534 0336 6 (paperback)

Printed in India

SPORTS
STORIES

CHOSEN BY
ALAN DURANT

ILLUSTRATED BY
DAVID KEARNEY

KING*f*ISHER

CONTENTS

INTRODUCTION

I LOVE SPORT and I love reading about it – I always have – and if you're reading this, then I guess you do too. Sport plays an important part in our lives, whether as participant or supporter, on or off the field of play, which is why sports stories have such resonance. At its best, sport is enthralling, dramatic and exciting, it puts you through the emotional mill and leaves you gasping but satisfied – and the best sports stories do much the same. In the best sports fiction, though, something is worked out, achieved, that goes beyond the mere winning of a trophy: self-esteem perhaps, respect, independence, friendship, loyalty, the playing out of shared hopes and dreams.

You'll find stories here about a wide variety of sports – from tennis to trolley-racing! Soccer, horse-racing, rugby, cricket, basketball, American football, athletics, swimming, baseball, ice hockey, cycling – all of these popular sports are represented. As to the trolley-racing, that's the activity described in the wonderful "Spit Nolan", which I've included as an example of street sport, the kind that's played spontaneously and without supervision. There are stories set in the past, present and future; about junior players and professionals – male and female; about teams and individuals. There are extracts from classic books, such as *Tom Brown's School Days*, and from the work of classic authors, such as P. G. Wodehouse. The long and universal appeal of the genre is reflected in the range of literary styles and stories here – from *The Iliad* to *Roy of the Rovers*!

As well as providing gripping entertainment, the sports story is an excellent medium to deal with issues of substance: it gets to the heart of real-life drama. As a boy, I was an avid fan of the football stories of Michael Hardcastle. His stories – like those of his American counterpart, Matt Christopher – are classic examples of the sort that mix exciting sporting action with a thought-provoking personal or social issue. In "Talk Us Through It", the issue is literally one of life or death – as it is in the acclaimed author Julius Lester's *Basketball Game*, which tackles the volatile issue of racial bigotry. Daughters' rights and sporting equality for girls are at stake in Will Weaver's feisty "Stealing for Girls", while the balance of individuality and teamwork is at the core of Walter Dean Myers' award-winning *Slam!* This combination of absorbing on-field action and strong emotional content is present in all of my favourite sports stories, and is what most draws me to the genre.

The writers included here have approached their subject in a variety of ways, but common to all is a real passion at the heart of their storytelling. You feel these writers have really experienced the profound thrill of sporting participation – at whatever level. Nowhere is that more striking than with Tessa Duder – an Olympic swimmer herself, she conveys the excitement of competition with gripping intensity in *Alex*. At the other end of the scale, my own story, "On Top of the World", is based on my still vivid memories of cross-country running at school. But the sports story can also be born of the imagination. Malorie Blackman's "Contact", for example, is a brilliantly imagined vision of a future in which virtual reality has replaced actual physical sport, while Philippa Pearce's "The Running-Companion" is a chilling account of relentless hatred and where this can lead.

One of the joys of putting together an anthology is rediscovering old favourites; another is discovering new ones, like the cycling story "Wet Bob, Dry Bob" by John Branfield. For this discovery (as for so much else) I have to thank my editor at Kingfisher, Caroline Edgley. With her help, I've assembled a line-up of talented individuals – from both sides of the Atlantic – that I hope you'll agree would make any team proud! Each of their stories captures the anticipation, adrenalin and excitement of sport, and will, I feel sure, give great and lasting satisfaction. And, what's more, you – the reader – won't have to work up a sweat to get it!

ALAN DURANT
May 2000

THE ILIAD

Retold by ALAN DURANT

The Iliad is thought to have been written in the eighth century BC. Attributed to a blind poet named Homer, it describes the bitter war between the Greeks and the Trojans. The poem also contains one of the earliest accounts of organised sporting competition – the funeral games held in honour of the slain Greek hero Patroclus. Many of the sports featured would have been part of the ancient Olympic Games, which were held every four years from 776 BC at the sacred site of Olympia in Greece. Running, the discus, the javelin, boxing, archery and wrestling are all still part of the modern Olympic Games, while the chariot race with its reckless manoeuvres has echoes of the highly competitive Formula 1 races of today. There's even a post-race inquiry – and a hint of crowd trouble, too!

AFTER THE FUNERAL of his beloved friend Patroclus, Achilles decided to hold a series of sporting games in his honour. The first event, he announced, was to be a chariot race and was open to all.

"Come forward and take your places!" he exhorted.

The first to enter was Eumelus, who was an expert horseman. Diomedes followed him with Menelaus, Antilochus and Meriones completing the field. Each man prepared and harnessed his chariot. Having drawn lots for starting positions, the charioteers lined up side by side for the start.

All at once, with a flick of their whips and a shake of their reins, they were off! The horses raced away across the plain, kicking up a storm of dust, their manes flowing in the wind. Behind them, the chariots bumped and bounced over the ground. The riders themselves stood tall, hearts thumping, as they urged their horses on.

It wasn't until the galloping horses had reached the turning post that was the halfway marker, and they were heading back towards the start, that the field started to spread. The speedy mares of Eumelus were the first to show, pulling away from the pack with Diomedes' team close behind – so close that Eumelus could feel the breath of the pursuing horses on his shoulders. Indeed, Diomedes would surely have overtaken Eumelus right there and then had the god Phoebus Apollo (who bore Diomedes a grudge) not knocked the whip from his hand, leaving him helpless. Seeing his rival race clear, Diomedes howled with rage and frustration. But help was at hand in the form of the goddess Athene. She retrieved Diomedes' whip and put fresh spirit in his horses. Moreover, she was so annoyed with Apollo that she chased Eumelus and unyoked his chariot's harness, so that his mares ran free. The chariot shaft slammed against the ground, throwing Eumelus from his chariot and almost under the wheels. His face was a mess of cuts and bruises and his eyes filled with tears. Meanwhile, Diomedes swept past at a clattering pace, leaving the rest of the field trailing in his wake.

The experienced Menelaus came next, followed by young Antilochus, who was shouting at his horses to quicken their pace and catch the team in front of them. The track ahead narrowed in a deep gully, wide enough for only one chariot to pass through, but Antilochus was determined to overtake Menelaus. Now he saw his opportunity. Instead of keeping to the track, he drove a little to one side, pushing Menelaus hard. The older man was alarmed.

"Rein in your horses, Antilochus! You're driving like a madman!" he cried. "You'll wreck both our chariots, if you keep that up."

But Antilochus pretended he couldn't hear and drove his horses on more recklessly than ever. Briefly, the two chariots

raced on, neither giving way until, finally, Menelaus dropped back for fear that the two chariots would collide and send their riders tumbling. "You'll answer for this, you lunatic!" Menelaus roared after Antilochus. "You're the worst driver in the world!"

There was also some discord among the spectators. The Cretan King Idomeneus had the best vantage point and he identified the leader as Diomedes. But Ajax disagreed. He accused Idomeneus of showing off.

"Your eyes aren't sharp enough to see that far," he remarked tartly. "You've got it all wrong. Eumelus is out in front."

The argument grew more heated and the two men might have come to blows had Achilles not intervened.

"Sit down and watch the race," he commanded. "The horses will be here any moment and then you'll recognize the leader right enough."

The leader, Diomedes, was now very close indeed. Flailing his whip, he drove his horses on towards the finish. They glided over the ground so swiftly that the golden chariot they pulled scarcely left a mark in the dust. They drew up in the middle of the arena, sweat pouring from their necks and chests. Diomedes leapt down from the vehicle in triumph.

The next to finish was Antilochus, with Menelaus hot on his heels. A spear's throw behind came Mariones, while Eumelus, the best driver of all, trailed in last, dragging his fine chariot himself. Feeling sorry for the unfortunate man, Achilles offered him a special consolation prize, which cheered Eumelus up considerably. Menelaus, on the other hand, was far from happy. He hadn't forgiven Antilochus for his dangerous manoeuvres and demanded an inquiry.

"Stand before your chariot now," he ordered Antilochus, "and swear that you didn't deliberately impede my chariot." He was in a foul mood. But Antilochus was quick to seek forgiveness.

"I broke the rules and I'm sorry," he apologised. "I willingly give you my prize." After this sporting gesture, the incident was soon forgotten.

When the prize-giving and speeches were done, Achilles stood up and announced the next event – a boxing match – and called for two worthy contenders to step forward. The call was answered at once by Epeus, who was a champion boxer.

"I'm the best boxer here," he declared, "and anyone who wants to stand against me had better have his mourners standing by, because I'm going to kill him!"

His challenge was met by complete silence. No one, it seemed, dared take it up. Then brave Euryalus walked into the ring. Diomedes acted as his second, binding his hands with specially-made oxhide thongs. When the two men were dressed and ready, they stepped into the middle of the ring and, raising their mighty fists, began to box. Fist pummelled fist. There was a terrible grinding of jaws; sweat streamed from their limbs. After a while, Euryalus momentarily lost concentration and, seeing his chance, Epeus delivered the knock-out punch to his opponent's chin. Euryalus's legs buckled beneath him, and he fell. A true sportsman, Epeus immediately gave his opponent a hand and helped him to his feet. Then Euryalus's followers supported him, as he staggered across the ring, head lolling, spitting blood. He was barely conscious when they sat him down in his corner.

No sooner had the boxing ended than Achilles introduced the third event – all-in wrestling – asking for two entrants. Without delay, the athletic Ajax got up and so too did wily Ulysses. They put on their shorts and stepped into the middle of the ring. As they each took hold of the other, they looked like a pair of solid sloping rafters. Their backs strained under the pressure of their strong hands. Sweat poured from their bodies. Red weals appeared on their sides and shoulders as they tussled – neither able to pin the other down. Eventually, realizing the crowd was growing restless, Ajax attempted to break the stalemate with a throw. He lifted Ulysses off his feet, but Ulysses retaliated with a kick to the hollow of his opponent's knee. As Ajax faltered, Ulysses flung him back and fell on his chest. The crowed roared, all shouting encouragement to the fighter they favoured.

Now it was Ulysses' turn to try a throw. He lifted Ajax a little, but he couldn't throw him. So he crooked his leg around Ajax's knee and brought him down again. They both fell, cheek by jowl, rolling in the dust. Then they jumped up and would have gone at it once more if Achilles had not intervened, declaring the contest a draw.

"Enough," he said. "You'll wear yourselves out and there are other contests to come."

The next event was the running race. There were three contestants: Ajax and Ulysses again – and the fastest of the younger men, Antilochus. The three of them lined up and Achilles pointed out the turning post, which marked halfway.

They were off like a shot! Ajax quickly took the lead, but Ulysses was close behind. There was so little between them that the dust had no time to settle in Ajax's footprints before Ulysses ran through them, his breath fanning the leader's head. Urged on by the shouts of his supporters, Ulysses strained every nerve to try to catch Ajax. As the two men neared the finish, Ulysses offered up a silent prayer to the goddess Athene.

"Help me, goddess," he prayed, "I need your help. Quicken my feet." Athene answered his prayer, lightening all his limbs. What's more, she tripped Ajax, just metres before the finish. He fell headlong into a pile of cattle dung, while Ulysses ran on to win the race. Ajax got up to finish second, with Antilochus a distant third. Ajax cursed his bad luck, spitting out dung as he did so – much to the amusement of the spectators.

Achilles exchanged pleasantries with his friend Antilochus before bringing out the prizes for the next event: armed combat. The contest was to be between the two best fighting men, the winner being the first to draw blood. Ajax (once more) and Diomedes took up the challenge. They armed themselves, then advanced upon each other, looking so fierce that those watching held their breath. Three times they charged and lunged at each other. Ajax managed to pierce Diomedes' shield, but his flesh, protected by his breast plate, was untouched. Now it was Diomedes' turn. Thrusting repeatedly above the rim of his opponent's shield, he nicked Ajax's neck with his glittering spear point. A cry of horror went up from the crowd, who called upon the contestants to stop, fearing for the welfare of Ajax. Diomedes was acclaimed the winner.

Next, it was the discus. Four men entered the event:

14

Polypoetes, Leonteus, Ajax and Epeus. Epeus went first, hurling the discus with all his might. But the spectators laughed at his effort. Leonteus was next to throw, followed by Ajax who easily passed the marks of the other two. The winner, though, was Polypoetes, whose throw beat the rest of the field by a huge distance, drawing loud applause.

For the archery, Achilles set up a ship's mast and, as a target, tied a pigeon to it by the foot.

"The man who hits the pigeon is the winner," he proclaimed.

Teucer and Meriones were to be the archers. They drew lots and it fell to Teucer to shoot first. He let fly an arrow with impressive force but didn't hit the bird. Instead, his arrow struck the thin cord that tethered the bird, severing it, so that the pigeon flew free. The spectators roared. Without hesitation, Meriones snatched the bow from Teucer's hands and strung an arrow. He glanced up at the pigeon fluttering high in the sky and, as it circled, he took aim and fired. His arrow pierced the bird's wing, passed straight through and landed back in the earth at his feet. The spectators were lost in admiration.

The final event was to be the javelin. However, when Achilles saw the great king Agamemnon was preparing to participate – in competition with Meriones – he called off the contest.

"No one can compete with you," he said. "You're the champion when it comes to throwing the javelin."

Agamemnon accepted the decision and Achilles gave both him and Meriones a prize.

Spectators and contestants now dispersed, returning to their ships for supper and a good night's sleep. The funeral games had been a fitting tribute to the valiant Patroclus.

GOAL OF THE DAY

TOM TULLY

Roy of the Rovers made his first appearance in the pages of the comic Tiger *in 1954. His goal-scoring exploits made him legendary. Indeed, even today, a commentator may say "this is Roy of the Rovers stuff" when a player achieves some extraordinary – and unlikely – footballing feat. There's even a website dedicated to the Melchester Rovers star. This story sees Roy Race in the twilight of his career, now player-manager of his famous team. When I was young, I loved footballing stories – the imaginary professional teams became real while I read about them.*

R OY HAD TIMED HIS RUN TO PERFECTION. Accelerating past Johnny Dexter, the Melchester player-manager met Terry Spring's diagonal pass at the corner of the goal area. Without a pause in his stride, Roy unleashed a low, rasping cross-shot that left the Rovers' reserve 'keeper, Charlie Carter, clawing at thin air.

"All right, boss, I give up," Johnny grinned ruefully. "It's like trying to mark a chicken with three legs."

Johnny's exasperated gasp drew chuckles from the other players. The Rovers' "Hard Man" had been the main victim of Roy's stunning, four-goal display in the seven-a-side practice match; a performance as sharp as anything they had ever seen from one of the deadliest strikers in European club football.

"I feel almost sorry for Tynecaster," Terry Spring remarked loudly. "If he plays like this tomorrow afternoon, we can start celebrating now. That three hundredth goal is a dead cert."

Roy glanced sharply at the stocky, dark-haired midfielder. His mouth half-opened, as if framing an angry retort. Then he said curtly, "All right, we'll call it a day. And remember, I don't want anyone talking to the press; not about *goals*, anyway . . ."

"A bit touchy, isn't he?" grunted Steve "Nobby" Wootten, as Roy loped off towards the distant complex of changing-rooms. "If I'd scored two hundred and ninety-nine goals in my career . . ."

"You'd be making sure the whole world knew about it, eh, Nobby?"

Scooping practice balls into a net, Mervyn Wallace, the Rovers' coach, was working his way towards the main group of players. "Well, that's not Roy's way," he went on. "He's far too busy trying to run a Premier League club to concern himself with statistics."

"But three hundred goals, Merv," Terry Spring said. "You can't just *ignore* an achievement like that."

"Everyone's on about it," Johnny added.

"And it's driving Roy up the wall. He's already done two television interviews, and been swamped with mail from well-wishers. And if he doesn't score on Saturday, it'll just go on, and on, and on . . ."

"So what do we do, Merv?"

"Keep quiet about it," the coach told him, ". . . if that's humanly possible. And for goodness sake, don't start trying to set up goals for him on Saturday. It'll play havoc with our system, and that's *all* we need against an outfit like Tynecaster!"

Roy could imagine the gist of the conversation that was taking place behind him; and he was only too aware that he was on the brink of becoming a "living legend", as one of the newspapers had put it. Of course it would be great to get three hundred goals under his belt, but he couldn't allow that prospect to dominate his thoughts.

As a manager, he had responsibilities that far outweighed the business of getting his name into the record books. That special goal would come, soon enough, if they would all just get off his back.

Shouldering his six-feet-two-inches frame through the door of his office, Roy stopped dead as he realized that the chair behind his desk was occupied.

"Hello, hot-shot," Ben Galloway greeted him. "I saw the last part of the training session. Let's hope it was a taste of things to come."

"You never know, Ben," Roy smiled, relieved to see that his visitor was the Rovers' bluff, sandy-haired general manager, and not a news-hungry reporter, in search of yet another interview.

Ben, presumably, was here on club business, something that would take his mind off a certain milestone in his career.

"Should be a big crowd tomorrow," Ben Galloway was saying, beginning to fidget in his chair. "I wish we'd made it all-ticket now. I mean, this isn't just another, er . . . league game, is it, Roy?"

"Why isn't it, Ben?" Roy said guardedly. For the first time, he noticed that Ben was clutching a copy of the club programme. "Just what did you want to see me about?"

"Nothing in particular. I was just, er . . . wondering if you'd changed your mind about . . ."

"My three-hundredth goal? A message to the fans in the programme?"

"Just a few words, Roy." Galloway shot to his feet, waving the programme almost desperately. "It could be a big day for the club, as well as yourself."

"No!" Roy cut in angrily. "I've already told you, Ben, I'm not making a song and dance about this confounded goal. Maybe I'll knock something out after I've scored the infernal thing, but not now, and that's final!"

"But, Roy . . ."

Ben broke off as the office door clicked open and Eddy Jarvis came bustling into the room. A small, brisk, neatly-dressed man, Eddy ran the Rovers' lottery scheme almost single-handedly, and was obviously feeling very pleased with himself.

"Thought you might like to see the design for the new lottery tickets, gentlemen," he announced, spreading out a large sheet of design paper on Roy's desk. "Rather topical, as you might say."

The word "topical" flooded Ben Galloway with alarm, but Roy was already peering at the design. "That's *me* isn't it? Kicking *three* footballs at once."

"That's right, boss," Eddy said proudly. "It's the top prize, and dead simple to play. All the punter has to do is scratch off the three footballs, which will expose three different numbers; and if the numbers add up to exactly . . ."

"Let me guess, Eddy," Roy said, icily. "The prize-winning total wouldn't be . . . three hundred, would it?"

"Bingo," cried Eddy.

"I don't believe this." Roy was already on his way out of the room. "If you will excuse me, gentlemen, I think it's time I took a shower!"

As the door slammed behind the Rovers' manager, Eddy Jarvis raised his eyebrows questioningly at Ben.

"Well . . . I didn't think the design was *that* bad."

"It's OK, Eddy," Ben said heavily. "You just happened to pick the wrong winning number!"

For Roy, the soothing effect of a long, hot shower didn't last very long. Forewarned by Rachel that a couple of reporters were waiting for him outside, he was forced to climb a fence, sneak through the housing estate that adjoined the training ground, and catch a taxi to his home.

His wife, Penny, took one look at Roy's dusty, dishevelled figure, and made him a cup of coffee.

Roy drained it without a word, and then said, "My love, if you so much as mention the word *goal* . . ."

"Not guilty," Penny smiled, "although I can't speak for the rest of the family, I'm afraid," she added. "Di and Melanie are, of course, full of it, and your son seems on the point of blowing his little top."

"Rocky?"

Penny nodded. "He's up in his room. He's been there since he came home from school."

Roy's son, Roy Race Junior, had earned his nickname "Rocky" from the aggressive, front-running style which had brought him a glut of goals in school matches. He was also in his second season as a schoolboy trainee with the Rovers.

Roy found his son perched on the end of his bed, stabbing almost viciously at the controls of a football video-game.

"You look as if you're attacking it, rather than playing it," Roy said, through a minor bedlam of electronic pings and bleeps. "What's the problem, son? Is it all this fuss about my three-hundredth goal? Have the other kids been getting at you?"

"Not really, Dad," the boy grunted, switching off the video-unit. "Except for Grant Fowler. I almost punched his head in, today."

"Why, for goodness' sake?"

"He's always taking the mickey, just because my father is Roy Race. I'm not so bothered about that, but . . ."

"But, what?"

"Fowler reckons you'll be trying so hard to score your three-hundredth goal tomorrow, it'll turn the game into a sort of *Roy Race exhibition match*."

"With disastrous consequences for the Rovers, eh?" Roy was wondering how many other people would be thinking along the same lines. The fans, the Tynecaster players, perhaps even his own team-mates.

"Young Grant could have a point," he went on, "*if* I allowed myself to think of nothing else except hitting the back of the net. But that's not going to happen, Rocky."

"But you *are* going to try, aren't you, Dad? I mean, all my other mates will be there. They'll be *praying* for you to score."

"And what if I *don't* score?"

Roy half-closed his eyes. If his son said something about not being able to show his face at school on Monday . . .

"You can score it against Portdean on Tuesday night," Rocky said. "Or against North Vale next Saturday."

20

Roy opened his eyes to find his son grinning at him. "Are you sure you can wait that long?" he chuckled, ruffling the boy's hair. "For all we know, I might go half a dozen games without scoring."

"No you won't, Dad. Mum says you're definitely going to score tomorrow."

"Your mother knows everything." Anxious to change the subject, Roy picked up the video-game.

"Anyway, young man, let's see if you've got *your* shooting boots on. I'll bet you fifty pence I can score more goals than you in three minutes."

"Go for it!" Rocky yelled.

Roy arrived at Mel Park the following morning, hoping that he would perform better against Tynecaster than he had against his son's video skills.

Rovers' famous, all-seater stadium was totally deserted except for a couple of groundsmen, putting finishing touches to the pitch markings. Roy had driven to the ground an hour earlier than usual, in the hope of avoiding the local newspaper "hounds". But a couple of reporters had anticipated his early arrival.

Flash cameras popped, and yells of "How do you feel, Roy? Gonna grab that golden goal today?" followed Roy as he dashed through the officials' carpark, and into the stadium.

A member of the office staff greeted him with a hesitant "Morning, boss."

Others merely nodded, smiled and muttered, "Good luck, Roy." No one actually mentioned goals.

But Roy could feel his stomach tightening as he walked into the Rovers' changing-room, where thirteen sets of red-and-yellow strip hung neatly around the walls.

Someone had left a stack of match programmes on a bench. He opened one of them at the centre-spread, and scanned the names of the players who would face the might of Tynecaster United . . .

N. HARDISTY
S. WOOTTEN   D. CHAPMAN
K. BRUCKNER   J. DEXTER
T. SPRING   R. RACE   K. CLARK
W. HARPER   A. MacCLAREN   M. CROKER
Substitutes: G. GUNN   A. RICHIE

It was a superb squad of peak-fit athletes: a team still in the running for winning the Premier League Championship.

Three points today, Roy reflected, would be far more important than the goal that everyone wanted him to score.

He was still flicking through the programme when Debbie Foster, the Rovers' physiotherapist arrived, closely followed by the first of the players.

"Any danger of the rocket going off today, boss?" Debbie inquired impishly. She was referring to "Racey's Rocket". Usually delivered with Roy's left foot from any angle, the "Rocket" was feared and respected throughout the league.

"If it does, physio, don't blink," was all Roy said. "Or you might miss it."

Catching a warning glance from Mervyn Wallace, Debbie left it at that.

The players changed in an atmosphere that almost crackled with tension. All of a sudden, Roy wanted to get out there: to get it over with. The number "300" was pounding in his brain, when the match referee, Ian Hughes, came in to brief the players about offsides, and free kicks.

As he was leaving, the official brandished the match ball at Roy.

"All the best, Racey," Hughes grinned. "I suppose we'll have to present you with this if you get your name on the score-sheet."

Hughes vanished before Roy could muster a reply. He turned, and looked at Mervyn Wallace.

"There's just no escape from it, is there?"

"Not for the next two hours, boss," the coach shrugged. He paused, listening to the muted hubbub of the crowd which had crammed itself into Mel Park.

"Quite apart from us, a few people out there are hoping that you're going to do it. Over forty-five thousand of them!"

Mervyn Wallace was right. Five minutes later, the mightiest roar he had ever heard engulfed Roy Race as he led out the Rovers.

"RACEY! RACEY!" came the thundering chant, rolling down from the vast flanks of the stadium.

The clamour increased during the warm-up. Each time Roy tucked a practice shot past Rapper Hardisty, a rapturous cheer greeted the "goal".

"SAVE IT FOR TYNECASTER, ROY!"

"WE WANT THREE HUNDRED! WE WANT THREE HUNDRED!"

"You'll be lucky," grunted Brian Hendry, the Tynecaster captain, as he and Roy shook hands at the centre spot. "Roy, if you want that three-hundredth goal, you'll have to sweat for it."

"Fair enough, Brian."

Roy had no intention of sweating for anything, except outright victory for the Rovers. But he had a hunch that the opposition might think differently: that he would be going all out to notch that precious goal.

His hunch proved right. Soon after the kick-off he realized that both Hendry and Danny Treacher – the United number six – had been ordered to mark him.

Just the job, Roy told himself. Heavy marking suited the particular tactics he had in mind. The game might develop into a Roy Race "spectacular", but not in the way that everyone was expecting.

Roy began to move deeper and deeper into his own half, drawing his shadowers with him. With the Rovers resisting the urge to feed the ball to him at every opportunity, and Tynecaster contenting themselves with cautious, probing attacks, the game was threatening to develop into a boring, midfield duel.

The crowd's impatience was building into a restless buzz, when Terry Spring – exchanging passes with Karl Bruckner – broke out of defence.

"Racey wants it!"

Even as Roy called sharply for the ball, he was on the move.

23

The fans exploded into life as he went surging down Rovers' right flank. His blistering speed left Hendry a pace or two behind him, and Bruckner's pass, when it came, was spot on.

As Danny Treacher loomed ahead of him, Roy feinted to go outside the man, slipped the ball between Treacher's splayed legs, and cut inside him. A perfect "nutmeg".

Suddenly, United's goal was only fifteen metres away, and the Melchester fans were on their feet.

"Go on, Roy, have a go!"

"BURY IT!"

The goal lay at an angle to him, but Roy had scored from such a position many times before. A low, accurate shot, just inside the near post and he and the fans could start celebrating.

The Tynecaster 'keeper was bracing himself for the expected hammer blow, as Roy hooked his right foot around the ball, and chipped it delicately across the penalty-area. The curving cross eluded a leaping defender, and homed in on the head of Kevin Clark, as he came thrusting in at the far post.

From such a range, the Rovers' "poacher" rarely missed.

"YESSSSSSSSS!"

"Nice one, boss," Kevin gasped, as he and Roy were mobbed by a crush of delighted colleagues. "But you left that cross a bit late. We all thought you were going to try one."

I *was*, Roy thought guiltily. For a split-second, the temptation to shoot for goal had been overwhelming and he realized, with a tingle of shock, that he wanted that three-hundredth goal as much as anyone in the stadium.

But, unless a certain scoring opportunity came his way, it would have to wait. All that mattered was beating Tynecaster.

Closing his mind to the shouts of "Your turn next, Roy," he began to drag his markers all over the pitch, creating a string of openings for his team-mates. He was a mere spectator when Johnny Dexter made one of his devastating raids down the left flank, and forced the United 'keeper into a fumbled save. The rebound was snapped up by Andy MacClaren . . .

"TWO–NIL," howled the fans, as the big Scot lifted the back of the net from close range.

By half-time, Rovers were in almost total command. "Tynecaster are falling into their own trap," Roy told his players during the interval. "They're so worried about me, they're leaving gaps you could drive a bus through; gaps that you lot can exploit!"

Roy's tactics were working so well, he became a human target for the visitors' frustration. Twenty minutes into the second half, a string of niggling fouls by Hendry and Treacher culminated in Hendry receiving a yellow card, and Rovers being awarded a direct free kick just outside the penalty-box.

"This time, Racey," begged the crowd. "GIVE 'EM THE ROCKET!"

Almost every Tynecaster player had crammed himself into the defensive "wall" . . . but the "rocket" never came.

Stepping over the ball at the last second, Roy allowed Terry Spring to dart in behind him and float a perfectly-weighted pass over the right flank of the wall. It was picked up by Wes Harper. Closing in, the black winger found the net with a low, angled drive that lashed under the 'keeper's body.

Melchester Rovers three, Tynecaster United nil.

By now, the fans' frantic demands for Roy to score himself were almost incessant.

"WE WANT THREE HUNDRED! WE WANT THREE HUNDRED!"

But Roy was far too busy avoiding the desperate tackles of the Tynecaster defenders. His legs were patterned with bruises by the time one of Rapper Hardisty's notorious "up-and-under" clearances caused utter havoc in the visitors' goal-mouth.

Caught in the furious scramble for the loose ball, Roy felt Danny Treacher's shoulder slam into the small of his back, hurling him off balance. As he staggered forward, something exploded against the side of his face. Only vaguely aware that he had collided with one of the uprights, Roy would have slumped to the turf if Andy MacClaren hadn't caught him.

"Roy, are you OK? Do you want the physio?"

Roy shook his head. His right temple was throbbing, and he felt curiously detached from the uproar around him.

"How much longer to go, Mac?"

"Couple of minutes, maybe less."

"Not worth getting Debbie off her stool," Roy muttered. He forced a grin at the hovering referee. "Might as well see it through, Ian."

"If you're sure, Roy . . ."

Ian Hughes had already awarded a corner to the Rovers. He watched closely as Roy walked away, a hand still clutched to his head, but reasonably steady on his feet now. Satisfied that the Melchester player-manager had recovered, Hughes gave the signal for the corner-kick to be taken.

It was one of Gary Gunn's specials: a wicked in-swinger, curling in towards the goal. Hustled by the soaring bulk of Andy MacClaren, all the Tynecaster 'keeper could do was get a hand to the ball, and swat it away.

As the ball looped towards Roy, who had wandered out to the edge of the penalty-area, a voice cracked through the tumult of the crowd.

"IT'S YOURS, ROY . . . HIT IT!"

Roy looked up, eyes flaring open as if he was seeing the ball for the first time. His reaction was breathtaking: one that players and fans alike would never forget.

His body half-rolled in mid-air as he heaved himself off the turf, his left leg lashing round like a flesh-and-bone scythe. Struck with perfect timing, and irresistible power, the ball streaked through a forest of players, hammered against the underside of the crossbar, and rebounded down into the net before the Tynecaster 'keeper could even make a move . . .

"HE'S DONE IT! IT'S THERRRRRE!"

Hardly anyone in the crowd heard the full time whistle, or even cared that Rovers had won four-nil. Roy collected a lot more bruises from the countless hands that pummelled his back all the way along the tunnel and down into the chaos of the changing-room.

Young Rocky was there, telling the world that his father was the greatest. Well-wishers swarmed in the corridors, and champagne was already sloshing into plastic beakers.

"What a showman," Ben Galloway laughed. "He plays will-o'-the-wisp with United for almost the whole game, and then . . . WHAM! Three hundred of the best!"

"Pure Melchester Magic," Rocky cried. "You timed it perfectly, Dad!"

"No I didn't," Roy said. "Well, *not deliberately*, anyway."

As they all stopped laughing, and chattering, and looked at him, Roy went on. "That argument with the upright shook me up more than I realized. I hardly knew what was happening, until someone yelled 'Hit it, Racey'."

"That . . . that was me," Terry Spring said faintly, "and you *did*."

"Without even *thinking* about it," Roy said. He shrugged, and grinned at the wide-eyed Rovers. "For all I knew at the time, it might have been my *1,000th* goal."

"Well, I'll be . . ." Ben Galloway's voice trailed into astonished silence. Like everyone else, he realized that he had just witnessed a piece of sublime opportunism: a history-making goal, fashioned from a split-second of sheer instinct.

"Roy," Debbie Foster hurried into the room, flushed with excitement, "the fans won't go home. They're calling for you to run a lap of honour."

The Rovers' player-manager frowned. He seemed about to refuse, when Mervyn Wallace said quietly, "Why not, boss? You've always said that the *fans* are what football's all about, not records and statistics."

The Rovers' coach eased his boss towards the door.

"Go on . . . share your glory with them. They deserve it."

Roy could hear the muffled roars now, vibrating down the tunnel.

"We want Racey! We want Racey!"

Mervyn's right, he thought. That goal belonged to all those people out there as much as to the record books.

As he turned into the tunnel, Ian Hughes stepped forward, and handed the match ball to him.

"Yours, I think, young man. I reckon you've earned it."

And then, his stride quickening, the "King" of Melchester went out to greet his subjects.

NATIONAL VELVET

ENID BAGNOLD

Written in 1935, National Velvet *is the most famous horse-racing story in fiction. Also a classic film starring Elizabeth Taylor, it depicts the exploits of teenage horsewoman Violet Browne, who enters the Grand National disguised as a male jockey (at that time female jockeys were not allowed to ride in the race). What makes this description of the race so memorable is the way it is viewed not from the perspective of the competitor, Violet, but from that of the horse's trainer, Mi, who struggles to follow the race among the crowds of spectators.*

AT THE POST THE TWENTY HORSES were swaying like the sea. Forward . . . No good! Back again. Forward . . . No good! Back again.

The line formed . . . and rebroke. Waves of the sea. Drawing a breath . . . breaking. Velvet fifth from the rail, between a bay and a brown. The Starter had long finished his instructions. Nothing more was said aloud, but low oaths flew, the cursing and grumbling flashed like a storm. An eye glanced at her with a look of hate. The breaking of movement was too close to movement to be borne. It was like water clinging to the tilted rim of the glass, like the sound of the dreaded explosion after the great shell has fallen. The will to surge forward overlaid by something delicate and terrible and strong, human obedience at bursting-point, but not broken. Horses' eyes gleamed openly, men's eyes set like chips of steel. Rough man, checked in violence, barely master of himself, barely master of his horse. The Piebald ominously quiet, and nothing coming from him . . . up went the tape.

The green Course poured in a river before her as she lay forward, and with the plunge of movement sat in the stream.

"Black slugs" . . . said Mi, cursing under his breath, running, dodging, suffocated with the crowd. It was the one thing he had overlooked, that the crowd was too dense ever to allow him to reach Becher's in the time. Away up above him was the truck-line, his once-glorious free seat, separated from him by a fence. "God's liver . . ." he mumbled, his throat gone cold, and stumbled into an old fool in a mackintosh. "Are they off?" he yelled at the heavy crowd as he ran, but no one bothered with him.

He was cursed if he was heeded at all. He ran, gauging his position by the cranes on the embankment. Velvet coming over Becher's in a minute and he not there to see her. "They're off." All around him a sea of throats offered up the gasp.

He was opposite Becher's but could see nothing: the crowd thirty deep between him and the Course. All around fell the terrible silence of expectancy. Mi stood like a rock. If he could not see them he must use his ears, hear. Enclosed in the dense, silent, dripping pack he heard the thunder coming. It roared up on the wet turf like the single approach of a multiple-footed animal. There were stifled exclamations, grunts, thuds. Something in the air flashed and descended. The first over Becher's! A roar went up from the crowd, then silence. The things flashing in the air were indistinguishable. The tip of a cap exposed for the briefest of seconds. The race went by like an express train, and was gone. Could Velvet be alive in that?

Sweat ran off Mi's forehead and into his eyes. But it was not sweat that turned the air grey and blotted out the faces before him. The ground on all sides seemed to be smoking. An extraordinary mist, like a low prairie fire was formed in the air. It had dwelt heavily all day behind the Canal, but the whole of the Course had remained clear till now. And now, before you could turn to look at your neighbour, his face was gone. The mist blew in shreds, drifted, left the crowd clear again but hid the whole of the Canal Corner, fences, stand and horses.

There was a struggle going on at Becher's; a horse had fallen and was being got out with ropes. Mi's legs turned to water and he asked his neighbour gruffly "who's fallen?" But the neighbour, straining to the tip of his toes, and glued to his glasses, was deaf as lead.

Suddenly Mi lashed round him in a frenzy. "Who's fallen, I say? Who's hurt!"

"Steady on," said a little man whom he had prodded in the stomach.

"Who's fallen?" said Mi desperately. "I gotta brother in this . . ."

"It's his brother!" said the crowd all around him. "Let him through."

Mi was pushed and pummelled to the front and remained embedded two from the front line. The horse that had fallen was a black horse, its neck unnaturally stretched by the ropes that were hauling it from the ditch.

There was a shout and a horse, not riderless, but ridden by a tugging, cursing man, came galloping back through the curling fumes of the mist, rolled its wild eye at the wrong side of Becher's and disappeared away out of the Course. An uproar began along the fringes of the crowd and rolled back to where Mi stood. Two more horses came back out of the mist, one riderless. The shades of others could be discerned in the fog. Curses rapped out from unseen mouths.

"What's happened at the Canal Turn? What's wrong down at the Turn?"

"The whole field!" shouted a man. The crowd took it up.

"The field's out. The whole field's come back. There's no race!" It was unearthly. Something a hundred yards down there in the fog had risen up and destroyed the greatest steeplechase in the world.

Nineteen horses had streamed down to the Canal Turn, and suddenly, there across the Course, at the boundary of the fog, four horses appeared beyond Valentine's, and among them, fourth, was The Piebald.

"Yer little lovely, yer little lovely!" yelled Mi, wringing his hands and hitting his knees. "It's her, it's him, it's me brother!"

No one took any notice. The scene immediately before them occupied all the attention. Horses that had fallen galloped by riderless, stirrups flying from their saddles, jockeys returned on foot, covered with mud, limping, holding their sides, some running slowly and miserably over the soggy course, trying to catch and sort the horses.

"It's 'Yellow Messenger'," said a jockey savagely, who had just seized his horse. "Stuck on the fence down there and kicking hell." And he mounted.

"And wouldn't they jump over him?" called a girl shrilly.

"They didn't wanter hurt the por thing, lady," said the jockey, grinning through his mud, and rode off.

"Whole lot piled up and refused," said a man who came up the line. "Get the Course clear now, quick!"

"They're coming again!" yelled Mi, watching the galloping four. "Get the Course clear! They'll be coming!"

They were out of his vision now, stuck down under Becher's high fence as he was. Once past Becher's on the second round would he have time to extricate himself and get back to the post before they were home? He stood indecisively and a minute went by. The Course in front of him was clear. Horses and men had melted. The hush of anticipation began to fall. "They're on the tan again," said a single voice. Mi flashed to a decision. He could not afford the minutes to be at Becher's. He must get back for the finish and it would take him all his time. He backed and plunged and ducked, got cursed afresh. The thunder was coming again as he reached the road and turned to face the far-off Stands. This time he could see nothing at all, not even a cap in the air. "What's leading? What's leading?"

"Big brown. Tantibus, Tantibus. Tantibus leading."

"Where's The Piebald?"

"See that! Leonora coming up . . ."

They were deaf to his frantic questions. He could not wait, but ran. This mist was ahead of him again, driving in frills and wafting sedgily about. Could Velvet have survived Becher's

33

twice? In any case no good wondering. He couldn't get at her to help her. If she fell he would find her more quickly at the hospital door. Better that than struggle through the crowd and be forbidden the now empty Course.

Then a yell. "There's one down!"

"It's the Yank mare!"

The horse ambulance was trundling back with Yellow Messenger from the Canal Turn. Mi leapt for a second on to the turning hub of the wheel, and saw in a flash, across the momentarily mist-clear course, the pride of Baltimore in the mud underneath Valentine's. The Piebald was lying third. The wheel turned and he could see no more. Five fences from the finish; he would not allow himself to hope, but ran and ran. How far away the Stands in the gaps of the mist as he pushed, gasping, through the people. Would she fall now? What had he done, bringing her up here? But would she fall now? He ran and ran.

"They're coming on to the Racecourse . . . coming on to the Racecourse . . ."

"How many?"

"Rain, rain, can't see a thing."

"How many?"

Down sank the fog again, as a puff of wind blew and gathered it together. There was a steady roaring from the Stands, then silence, then a hubbub. No one could see the telegraph.

Mi, running, gasped. "Who's won?"

But everyone was asking the same question. Men were running, pushing, running, just as he. He came up to the gates of Melling Road, crossed the road on the fringe of the tan, and suddenly, out of the mist The Piebald galloped riderless, lolloping unsteadily along, reins hanging, stirrups dangling. Mi burst through on to the Course, his heart wrung.

"Get back there!" shouted a policeman. "Loose horse!"

"Hello Old Pie there!" shouted Mi. The animal, soaked, panting, spent, staggered and slipped and drew up.

"What've you done with 'er?" said Mi weeping, and bent down to lift the hoof back through the rein. "You let 'er down, Pie? What in God's sake?" He led the horse down the Course, running, his

34

breath catching, his heart thumping, tears and rain on his face.

"Two men came towards him out of the mist.

"You got him?" shouted one. "Good for you. Gimme!"

"You want him?" said Mi, in a stupor, giving up the rein.

"Raised an objection. Want him for the enclosure. Chap come queer."

"Chap did? What chap?"

"This here's the winner! Where you bin all day, Percy?"

"Foggy," said Mi. "Very foggy. Oh my God!"

Back in the fog a voice had spoken into a telephone. It had need only to say one word. All else had been written out beforehand. And in that very second in the offices of the Associated Press in New York men had taken off the message.

"Urgent Associated New York Flash Piebald Wins." The one word the voice had said into the fog was "Piebald".

Up went the red flag. The crowd buzzed. "What is it?" "Did he fall?"

"Must've hurt hisself jumping . . ."

"Fainted."

"Jus' dismounted, the silly b . . ."

Dismounted before reaching the unsaddling enclosure. Objection. Up went the red flag. There was tenseness along the line of private bookies, pandemonium in the bookies' stand under the umbrellas, tight knots gathered round the opening to the Weighing Room, behind which was the Stewards' Room. Glasses were levelled from everywhere upon the board. If a white flag went up the objection was overruled. If a green it was sustained. But the red remained unwaveringly.

"Taken him round to the hospital."

"Stretcher, was it?"

"Jus' gone through where all those people are . . ."

The doctor had got back from his tour of the Course in his ambulance. Two riders had already been brought in and the nurse had prepared them in readiness for his examination. Now the winner himself coming in on a stretcher. Busy thirty minutes ahead.

"Get him ready, Sister."

The winner lay unconscious wrapped in a horse blanket, his face mottled with the mud that had leapt up from flying hooves.

"Looks sixteen," said the doctor curiously, and knelt to turn the gas a little lower under the forceps.

"Bin boiling for twenty minutes," said the Sister.

"Place full of steam," said the doctor. "Been watching . . .?" and he passed to the end cubicle.

"No," said the Sister shortly to his back. She disliked the Grand National, and had waited behind the Stands to patch up the damage.

The constables with the stretcher placed the winner on the bed by the door, leaving him still wrapped in his blanket. They retired and closed the door. The Sister slipped a towel under the muddy head, and turning back the blanket started to undo the soaking jacket of black silk.

"Sister," roared the doctor from another cubicle . . . "No, stay where you are! I've got it!"

"Could you come here a minute?" said the Sister, at his side a few minutes later.

The doctor straightened his back. He had a touch of lumbago. "I'll be back, Jem," he said. "You're not much hurt. Cover up. Yes?"

"Just a minute . . . over here."

She whispered to him quietly. He slapped his rain-coated cheek and went to the bed by the door. "Put your screens round." She planted them. "Constable," he said, poking his head out of the door, "get one of the Stewards here, will you." (The roar of the crowd came in at the door.) "One of the Stewards! Quick's you can. Here, I'll let you in this side door. You can get through." The crowd seethed, seizing upon every sign.

Mi crouched by the door without daring to ask after his child. He heard the doctor call. He saw the Steward go in. "Anyway," he thought, "they've found out at once. They would. What's it matter if she's all right? She's won, the little beggar, the little beggar. Oh my God!"

The Sergeant of Police was by the Stables. "Message from up there," he said briefly to his Second. "Squad to go up to the hospital door. Row round the door. Something up with the winner."

The police marched up in a black snake. The people fell back. An ambulance came in from the Ormskirk Road and backed down the line of police. The red flag remained for a moment, then slowly the green flag mounted on the board. Objection sustained. A frightful clamour burst out in the Grand Stand.

In the Stewards' Room the glittering Manifesto looked down out of his frame and heard the low talk of this appalling desecration. A butcher's girl on a piebald horse had pounced up beside him into history.

"Got her off?" said one of the Stewards in a low voice.

"Just about. There was a bit of a rush for a second. She called out something as the stretcher was being shoved in. Called out she was all right . . . to somebody in the crowd. Good God, it's . . . I'm glad we got her off quick. The crowd's boiling with excitement."

"How'd it get out so quick?"

"I dunno. Swell row this'll be. It'll have to be referred back to Weatherby's." The Clerk of the Course came in. "Crowd's bubbling like kettles out there, Lord Henry. By jove, it's the biggest ramp! How'd she pull it over?"

"Who's gone with her?"

"The doctor couldn't go. He's got two other men, one a baddish crash at Valentine's."

"Well somebody ought to a' gone. Find out who's gone, will you?"

The Clerk of the Course disappeared.

"Tim's Chance wins, of course."

"Yes, that's been announced. There's no question. The objection is sustained definitely here on the Course, and the rest must be referred to London. There'll be a special of the NHC, I should think it might be a case for legal proceedings. Well . . ." (as the door opened) "did you find out who went with her?"

"A second doctor, Lord Henry. A young man who's here very often. Friend of Doctor Bodie's. And a constable."

"There should have been an official. Of course there should have been an official. What's the hospital?"

"Liverpool Central . . ."

"Isn't there a friend or relation with her?"

"Nobody."

"Well, she called out to somebody!"

"The somebody's hidden himself all right. Well for him! She's quite alone s'far as we can make out."

"D'she say anything?"

"Won't speak. Except that one shout she gave."

"If my daughter'd done it," said Lord Henry Vile, "I'd be . . ." he paused and stroked his lip with his finger.

"Pretty upset, I should think . . ."

"I wasn't going to say that," said Lord Henry. "No."

JUST ONCE

THOMAS J. DYGARD

EVERYBODY LIKED THE MOOSE. To his father and mother he was Bryan – as in Bryan Jefferson Crawford – but to everyone at Bedford City High he was the Moose. He was large and strong, as you might imagine from his nickname, and he was pretty fast on his feet – sort of nimble, you might say – considering his size. He didn't have a pretty face but he had a quick and easy smile – "sweet," some of the teachers called it; "nice," others said.

But on the football field, the Moose was neither sweet nor nice. He was just strong and fast and a little bit devastating as the left tackle of the Bedford City Bears. When the Moose blocked somebody, he stayed blocked. When the Moose was called on to open a hole in the line for one of the Bears' runners, the hole more often than not resembled an open garage door.

Now in his senior season, the Moose had twice been named to the all-conference team and was considered a cinch for all-state. He spent a lot of his spare time, when he wasn't in a classroom or on the football field, reading letters from colleges eager to have the Moose pursue higher education – and football – at their institution.

But the Moose had a hang-up.

He didn't go public with his hang-up until the sixth game of the season. But, looking back, most of his team-mates agreed that probably the Moose had been nurturing the hang-up secretly for two years or more.

The Moose wanted to carry the ball.

For sure, the Moose was not the first interior lineman in the history of football, or even the history of Bedford City High, who banged heads up front and wore bruises like badges of honour – and dreamed of racing down the field with the ball to the end zone while everybody in the bleachers screamed his name.

But most linemen, it seems, are able to stifle the urge. The idea may pop into their minds from time to time, but in their hearts they know they can't run fast enough, they know they can't do that fancy dancing to elude tacklers, they know they aren't trained to read blocks. They know that their strengths and talents are best utilized in the line. Football is, after all, a team sport, and everyone plays the position where he most helps the team. And so these linemen, or most of them, go back to banging heads without saying the first word about the dream that flickered through their minds.

Not so with the Moose.

That sixth game, when the Moose's hang-up first came into public view, had ended with the Moose truly in all his glory as the Bears' left tackle. Yes, glory – but uncheered and sort of anonymous. The Bears were trailing 21–17 and had the ball on Mitchell High's five-yard line, fourth down, with time running out. The rule in such a situation is simple – the best back carries the ball behind the best blocker – and it is a rule seldom violated by those in control of their faculties. The Bears, of course, followed the rule. That meant Jerry Dixon running behind the Moose's blocking. With the snap of the ball, the Moose knocked down one lineman, bumped another one aside, and charged forward to flatten an approaching linebacker. Jerry did a little jig behind the Moose and then ran into the end zone, virtually untouched, to win the game.

After circling in the end zone a moment while the cheers echoed through the night, Jerry did run across and hug the Moose, that's true. Jerry knew who had made the touchdown possible.

But it wasn't the Moose's name that everybody was shouting. The fans in the bleachers were cheering Jerry Dixon.

It was probably at that precise moment that the Moose decided to go public.

In the dressing room, Coach Buford Williams was making his rounds among the cheering players and came to a halt in front of the Moose. "It was your great blocking that did it," he said.

"I want to carry the ball," the Moose said.

Coach Williams was already turning away and taking a step towards the next player due an accolade when his brain registered the fact that the Moose had said something strange. He was expecting the Moose to say, "Aw, gee; thanks, Coach." That was what the Moose always said when the coach issued a compliment. But the Moose had said something else. The coach turned back to the Moose, a look of disbelief on his face. "What did you say?"

"I want to carry the ball."

Coach Williams was good at quick recoveries, as any high-school football coach had better be. He gave a tolerant smile and a little nod and said, "You keep right on blocking, son."

This time Coach Williams made good on his turn and moved away from the Moose.

The following week's practice and the next Friday's game passed without further incident. After all, the game was a road game over at Cartwright High, thirty-five miles away. The Moose wanted to carry the ball in front of the Bedford City fans.

Then the Moose went to work.

He caught up with the coach on the way to the practice field on Wednesday. "Remember," he said, leaning forward and down a little to get his face in the coach's face, "I said I want to carry the ball."

Coach Williams must have been thinking about something else because it took him a minute to look up into the Moose's face, and even then he didn't say anything.

"I meant it," the Moose said.

"Meant what?"

"I want to run the ball."

"Oh," Coach Williams said. Yes, he remembered. "Son, you're a great left tackle, a great blocker. Let's leave it that way."

The Moose let the remaining days of the practice week and then the game on Friday night against Edgewood High pass while he reviewed strategies. The review led him to Dan Blevins, the Bears' quarterback. If the signal-caller would join in, maybe Coach Williams would listen.

"Yeah, I heard," Dan said. "But, look, what about Joe Wright at guard, Bill Slocum at right tackle, even Herbie Watson at centre. They might all want to carry the ball. What are we going to do – take turns? It doesn't work that way."

So much for Dan Blevins.

The Moose found that most of the players in the backfield agreed with Dan. They couldn't see any reason why the Moose should carry the ball, especially in place of themselves. Even Jerry Dixon, who owed a lot of his glory to the Moose's blocking, gaped in disbelief at the Moose's idea. The Moose, however, got some support from his fellow linemen. Maybe they had dreams of their own, and saw value in a precedent.

As the days went by, the word spread – not just on the practice field and in the corridors of Bedford City High, but all around town. The players by now were openly taking sides. Some thought it a jolly good idea that the Moose carry the ball. Others, like Dan Blevins, held to the purist line – a left tackle plays left tackle, a ballcarrier carries the ball, and that's it.

Around town, the vote wasn't even close. Everyone wanted the Moose to carry the ball.

"Look, son," Coach Williams said to the Moose on the practice field the Thursday before the Benton Heights game, "this has gone far enough. Fun is fun. A joke is a joke. But let's drop it."

"Just once," the Moose pleaded.

Coach Williams looked at the Moose and didn't answer.

The Moose didn't know what that meant.

The Benton Heights Tigers were duck soup for the Bears, as everyone knew they would be. The Bears scored in their first three possessions and led 28–0 at the half. The hapless Tigers had yet to cross the fifty-yard line under their own steam.

All the Bears, of course, were enjoying the way the game was going, as were the Bedford City fans jamming the bleachers.

Coach Williams looked irritated when the crowd on a couple of occasions broke into a chant: "Give the Moose the ball! Give the Moose the ball!"

On the field, the Moose did not know whether to grin at hearing his name shouted by the crowd or to frown because the sound of his name was irritating the coach. Was the crowd going to talk Coach Williams into putting the Moose in the backfield? Probably not; Coach Williams didn't bow to that kind of pressure. Was the coach going to refuse to give the ball to the Moose just to show the crowd – and the Moose and the rest of the players – who was boss? The Moose feared so.

In his time on the sideline, when the defensive unit was on the field, the Moose, of course, said nothing to Coach Williams. He knew better than to break the coach's concentration during a game – even a runaway victory – with a comment on any subject at all, much less his desire to carry the ball. As a matter of fact, the Moose was careful to stay out of the coach's line of vision, especially when the crowd was chanting "Give the Moose the ball!"

By the end of the third quarter the Bears were leading 42–0.

Coach Williams had been feeding substitutes into the game since half-time, but the Bears kept marching on. And now, in the opening minutes of the fourth quarter, the Moose and his team-mates were standing on the Tigers' five-yard line, about to pile on another touchdown.

The Moose saw his substitute, Larry Hinden, getting a slap on the behind and then running on to the field. The Moose turned to leave.

Then he heard Larry tell the referee, "Hinden for Holbrook."

Holbrook? Chad Holbrook, the fullback?

Chad gave the coach a funny look and jogged off the field.

Larry joined the huddle and said, "Coach says the Moose at fullback and give him the ball."

Dan Blevins said, "Really?"

"Really."

The Moose was giving his grin – "sweet," some of the teachers called it; "nice," others said.

"I want to do an end run," the Moose said.

Dan looked at the sky a moment, then said, "What does it matter?"

The quarterback took the snap from centre, moved back and to his right while turning, and extended the ball to the Moose.

The Moose took the ball and cradled it in his right hand. So far, so good. He hadn't fumbled. Probably both Coach Williams and Dan were surprised.

He ran a couple of steps and looked out in front and said aloud, "Whoa!"

Where had all those tacklers come from?

The whole world seemed to be peopled with players in red jerseys – the red of the Benton Heights Tigers. They were all looking straight at the Moose and advancing toward him. They looked determined, and not friendly at all. And there were so many of them. The Moose had faced tough guys in the line, but usually one at a time, or maybe two. But this – five or six. And all of them heading for him.

The Moose screeched to a halt, whirled, and ran the other way.

Dan Blevins blocked somebody in a red jersey breaking through the middle of the line, and the Moose wanted to stop running and thank him. But he kept going.

His reverse had caught the Tigers' defenders going the wrong way, and the field in front of the Moose looked open. But his blockers were going the wrong way, too. Maybe that was why the field looked so open. What did it matter, though, with the field clear in front of him? This was going to be a cakewalk; the Moose was going to score a touchdown.

Then, again – "Whoa!"

Players with red jerseys were beginning to fill the empty space – a lot of them. And they were all running towards the Moose. They were kind of low, with their arms spread, as if they wanted to hit him hard and then grab him.

A picture of Jerry Dixon dancing his little jig and wriggling between tacklers flashed through the Moose's mind. How did

Jerry do that? Well, no time to ponder that one right now.

The Moose lowered his shoulder and thundered ahead, into the cloud of red jerseys. Something hit his left thigh. It hurt. Then something pounded his hip, then his shoulder. They both hurt. Somebody was hanging on to him and was a terrible drag. How could he run with somebody hanging on to him? He knew he was going down, but maybe he was across the goal. He hit the ground hard, with somebody coming down on top of him, right on the small of his back.

The Moose couldn't move. They had him pinned. Wasn't the referee supposed to get these guys off?

Finally, the load was gone and the Moose, still holding the ball, got to his knees and one hand, then stood.

He heard the screaming of the crowd, and he saw the scoreboard blinking.

He had scored.

His team-mates were slapping him on the shoulder pads and laughing and shouting.

The Moose grinned, but he had a strange and distant look in his eyes.

He jogged to the sideline, the roars of the crowd still ringing in his ears.

"OK, son?" Coach Williams asked.

The Moose was puffing. He took a couple of deep breaths. He relived for a moment the first sight of a half dozen players in red jerseys, all with one target – him. He saw again the menacing horde of red jerseys that had risen up just when he'd thought he had clear sailing to the goal. They all zeroed in on him, the Moose, alone.

The Moose glanced at the coach, took another deep breath, and said, "Never again."

MIKE AT WRYKYN

P. G. WODEHOUSE

P. G. Wodehouse is best known for his humorous stories, featuring such classic comic characters as Jeeves and Wooster. This story features Mike Jackson, the youngest in a line of cricketing brothers, who gets his chance to play for his school, Wrykyn, when three of the usual eleven are put on detention. He plays alongside his brother Bob, while his eldest brother Joe, and his boyhood cricket tutor, Saunders, are both in the opposing MCC team. This evocative story, that I first read in my early teens, captures all the excitement and eccentricities of a school cricket match.

IF THE DAY HAPPENS TO BE FINE, there is a curious, dreamlike atmosphere about the opening stages of a first-eleven match. Everything seems hushed and expectant. The rest of the school have gone in after the interval at eleven o'clock, and you are alone on the ground with a cricket bag. The only signs of life are a few pedestrians on the road beyond the railings and one or two blazer and flannel-clad forms in the pavilion. The sense of isolation is trying to the nerves, and a school team usually bats twenty-five per cent better after lunch, when the strangeness has worn off.

Mike walked across from Wain's, where he had changed, feeling quite hollow. He could almost have cried with pure fright. Bob had shouted after him from a window as he passed

Donaldson's, to wait, so that they could walk over together; but conversation was the last thing Mike desired at that moment.

He had almost reached the pavilion when one of the MCC. team came down the steps, saw him, and stopped dead.

"By Jove, Saunders!" cried Mike.

"Why, Master Mike!"

The professional beamed, and quite suddenly, the lost, hopeless feeling left Mike. He felt cheerful as if he and Saunders had met in the meadow at home, and were just going to begin a little quiet net-practice.

"Why, Master Mike, you don't mean to say you're playing for the school already?"

Mike nodded happily.

"Isn't it terrific?" he said.

Saunders slapped his leg in a sort of ecstasy.

"Didn't I always say it, sir," he chuckled. "Wasn't I right? I used to say to myself it 'ud be a pretty good school team that 'ud leave you out."

"Of course, I'm only playing as a sub., you know. Three chaps are in extra, and I got one of the places."

"Well, you'll make a hundred today, Master Mike, and then they'll have to put you in."

"Wish I could!"

"Master Joe's come down with the Club," said Saunders.

"Joe! Has he really? How ripping! Hello, here he is. Hello, Joe?"

The greatest of all the Jacksons was descending the pavilion steps with the gravity befitting an All England batsman. He stopped short, as Saunders had done.

"Mike! You aren't playing!"

"Yes."

"Well, I'm hanged! Young marvel, isn't he, Saunders?"

"He is, sir," said Saunders. "Got all the strokes. I always said it, Master Joe. Only wants the strength."

Joe took Mike by the shoulder, and walked him off in the direction of a man in a Zingari blazer who was bowling slows to another of the MCC team. Mike recognized him with awe as one of the three best amateur wicket-keepers in the country.

"What do you think of this?" said Joe, exhibiting Mike, who grinned bashfully. "Aged fifteen last birthday, and playing for the school. You are only fifteen, aren't you, Mike?

"Brother of yours?" asked the wicket-keeper.

"Probably too proud to own the relationship, but he is."

"Isn't there any end to you Jacksons?" demanded the wicket-keeper in an aggrieved tone. "I never saw such a family."

"This is our star. You wait till he gets at us today. Saunders is our only bowler, and Mike's been brought up on Saunders. You'd better win the toss if you want a chance of getting a knock and lifting your average out of the minuses."

"I *have* won the toss," said the other with dignity. "Do you think I don't know the elementary duties of a captain?"

The school went out to field with mixed feelings. The wicket was hard and true, which would have made it pleasant to be going in first. On the other hand, they would feel decidedly better and fitter for centuries after the game had been in progress an hour or so. Burgess was glad as a private individual, sorry as a captain. For himself, the sooner he got hold of the ball and began to bowl the better he liked it. As a captain, he realized that a side with Joe Jackson in it, not to mention the other first-class men, was not a side to which he would have preferred to give away an advantage. Mike was feeling that by no possibility could he hold the simplest catch, and hoping that nothing would come his way. Bob, conscious of being an uncertain field, was feeling just the same.

The MCC opened with Joe and a man in an Oxford Authentic cap. The beginning of the game was quiet. Burgess's yorker was nearly too much for the latter in the first over, but he contrived to shop it away, and the pair gradually settled down. At twenty, Joe began to open his shoulders. Twenty became forty with disturbing swiftness, and Burgess tried a change of bowling.

It seemed for one instant as if the move had been a success, for Joe, still taking risks, tried to late-cut a rising ball, and snicked it straight into Bob's hands at second slip. It was the easiest of slip-catches, but Bob fumbled it, dropped it, almost held it a second time, and finally let it fall miserably to the ground. It was a moment too painful for words. He rolled the ball back to the bowler in silence.

One of those weary periods followed when the batsman's defence seems to the fieldsmen absolutely impregnable. There was a sickening inevitableness in the way in which every ball was played with the very centre of the bat. And, as usual, just when things seemed most hopeless, relief came. The Authentic, getting in front of his wicket, to pull one of the simplest long-hops ever seen on a cricket field, missed it, and was lbw. And the next ball upset the newcomer's leg stump.

The school revived. Bowlers and field were infused with a new life. Another wicket – two stumps knocked out of the ground by Burgess – helped the thing on. When the bell rang for the end of morning school, five wickets were down for a hundred and thirteen.

But from the end of school till lunch things went very wrong indeed. Joe was still in at one end, invincible; and at the other was the great wicket-keeper. And the pair of them suddenly began to force the pace till the bowling was in a tangled knot. Four after four, all round the wicket, with never a chance or a mishit to vary the monotony. Two hundred went up, and two hundred and fifty. Then Joe reached his century, and was stumped next ball. Then came lunch.

The rest of the innings was like the gentle rain after the thunderstorm. Runs came with fair regularity, but wickets fell at intervals, and when the wicket-keeper was run out at length for a lively sixty-three, the end was very near. Saunders, coming in last, hit two boundaries, and was then caught by Mike. His second hit had just lifted the MCC total over the three hundred.

Three hundred is a score that takes some making on any ground, but on a fine day it was not an unusual total for the Wrykyn eleven. Some years before, against Ripton, they had run up four-hundred-and-sixteen; and only last season had massacred a very weak team of Old Wrykynians with a score that only just missed the fourth hundred.

Unfortunately, on the present occasion, there was scarcely

time, unless the bowling happened to get completely collared, to make the runs. It was a quarter to four when the innings began, and stumps were to be drawn at a quarter to seven. A hundred an hour is quick work.

Burgess, however, was optimistic, as usual. "Better have a go for them," he said to Berridge and Marsh, the school first pair.

Following out this courageous advice, Berridge, after hitting three boundaries in his first two overs, was stumped halfway through the third.

After this, things settled down. Morris, the first-wicket man, was a thoroughly sound bat, a little on the slow side, but exceedingly hard to shift. He and Marsh proceeded to play themselves in, until it looked as if they were likely to stay till the drawing of stumps.

A comfortable, rather somnolent feeling settled upon the school. A long stand at cricket is a soothing sight to watch. There was an absence of hurry about the batsmen which harmonized well with the drowsy summer afternoon. And yet runs were coming at a fair pace. The hundred went up at five o'clock, the hundred and fifty at half-past. Both batsmen were completely at home, and the MCC third-change bowlers had been put on.

Then the great wicket-keeper took off the pads and gloves, and the fieldsmen retired to posts at the extreme edge of the ground.

"Lobs," said Burgess. "By Jove, I wish I was in."

It seemed to be the general opinion among the members of the Wrykyn eleven on the pavilion balcony that Morris and Marsh were in luck. The team did not grudge them their good fortune, because they had earned it; but they were distinctly envious.

Lobs are the most dangerous, insinuating things in the world. Everybody knows in theory the right way to treat them. Everybody knows that the man who is content not to try to score more than a single cannot get out to them. Yet nearly everybody does get out to them.

It was the same story today. The first over yielded six runs, all through gentle taps along the ground. In the second, Marsh hit an over-pitched one along the ground to the terrace bank.

The next ball he swept round to the leg boundary. And that was the end of Marsh. He saw himself scoring at the rate of twenty-four an over. Off the last ball he was stumped by several feet, having done himself credit by scoring seventy.

The long stand was followed, as usual, by a series of disasters. Marsh's wicket had fallen at a hundred and eighty. Ellerby left at a hundred and eighty-six. By the time the scoring-board registered two hundred, five wickets were down, three of them victims to the lobs. Morris was still in at one end. He had refused to be tempted. He was jogging on steadily to his century.

Bob Jackson went in next, with instructions to keep his eye on the lob-man.

For a time things went well. Saunders, who had gone on to bowl again after a rest, seemed to give Morris no trouble, and Bob put him through the slips with apparent ease. Twenty runs were added, when the lob-bowler once more got in his deadly work. Bob, letting alone a ball wide of the off-stump under the impression that it was going to break away, was disagreeably surprised to find it break in instead, and hit the wicket. The bowler smiled sadly, as if he hated to have to do these things.

Mike's heart jumped as he saw the bails go. It was his turn next.

"Two hundred and twenty-nine," said Burgess, "and it's ten past six. No good trying for the runs now. Stick in," he added to Mike. "That's all you've got to do."

All! . . . Mike felt as if he was being strangled. His heart was racing like the engines of a motor. He knew his teeth were chattering. He wished he could stop them. What a time Bob was taking to get back to the pavilion! He wanted to rush out, and get the thing over.

At last he arrived, and Mike, fumbling at a glove, tottered out into the sunshine. He heard miles and miles away a sound of clapping, and a thin, shrill noise as if somebody were screaming in the distance. As a matter of fact, several members of his form and the junior day-room at Wain's nearly burst themselves at that moment.

At the wickets, he felt better. Bob had fallen to the last ball of the over, and Morris, standing ready for Saunders' delivery, looked so calm and certain of himself that it was impossible to feel entirely without hope and self-confidence. Mike knew that Morris had made ninety-eight, and he supposed that Morris knew that he was very near his century; yet he seemed to be absolutely undisturbed. Mike drew courage from his attitude.

Morris pushed the first ball away to leg. Mike would have liked to have run two, but short leg had retrieved the ball as he reached the crease.

The moment had come, the moment which he had experienced only in dreams. And in the dreams he was always full of confidence, and invariably hit a boundary. Sometimes a drive, sometimes a cut, but always a boundary.

"To leg, sir," said the umpire.

"Don't be in a funk," said a voice. "Play straight, and you can't get out."

It was Joe, who had taken the gloves when the wicket-keeper went on to bowl.

Mike grinned, wryly but gratefully.

Saunders was beginning his run. It was all so home-like that for a moment Mike felt himself again. How often he had seen those two little skips and the jump. It was like being in the paddock again, with Marjory and the dogs waiting by the railings to fetch the ball if he made a drive.

Saunders ran to the crease, and bowled.

Now, Saunders was a conscientious man, and, doubtless, bowled the very best ball that he possibly could. On the other hand, it was Mike's first appearance for the school, and Saunders, besides being conscientious, was undoubtedly kind-hearted. It is useless to speculate as to whether he was trying to bowl his best that ball. If so, he failed signally. It was a half-volley, just the right distance from the off-stump; the sort of ball Mike was wont to send nearly through the net at home . . .

The next moment the dreams had come true. The umpire was signalling to the scoring-box, the school was shouting, extra-cover was trotting to the boundary to fetch the ball, and Mike was blushing and wondering whether it was bad form to grin.

From that ball onwards all was for the best in this best of all

possible worlds. Saunders bowled no more half-volleys; but Mike played everything that he did bowl. He met the lobs with a bat like a barn-door. Even the departure of Morris, caught in the slips off Saunders' next over for a chanceless hundred and five, did not disturb him. All nervousness had left him. He felt equal to the situation. Burgess came in, and began to hit out as if he meant to knock off the runs. The bowling became a shade loose. Twice he was given full tosses to leg, which he hit to the terrace bank. Half-past six chimed, and two hundred and fifty went up on the telegraph board. Burgess continued to hit. Mike's whole soul was concentrated on keeping up his wicket. There was only Reeves to follow him, and Reeves was a victim to the first straight ball. Burgess had to hit because it was the only game he knew; but he himself must simply stay in.

The hands of the clock seemed to have stopped. Then suddenly he heard the umpire say "Last over," and he settled down to keep those six balls out of his wicket.

The lob-bowler had taken himself off, and the Oxford Authentic had gone on, fast left-hand.

The first ball was short and wide of the off-stump. Mike let it alone. Number two: yorker. Got him! Three: straight half-volley. Mike played it back to the bowler. Four: beat him, and missed the wicket by an inch. Five: another yorker. Down on it again in the old familiar way.

All was well. The match was a draw now whatever happened to him. He hit out, almost at a venture, at the last ball, and mid-off, jumping, just failed to reach it. It hummed over his head, and ran like a streak along the turf and up the bank, and a great howl of delight went up from the school as the umpire took off the bails.

Mike walked away from the wicket with Joe and the wicket-keeper.

"I'm sorry about your nose, Joe," said the wicket-keeper in tones of grave solicitude.

"What's wrong with it?"

"At present," said the wicket-keeper, "nothing. But in a few years I'm afraid it's going to be put badly out of joint."

STEALING FOR GIRLS

WILL WEAVER

IT'S A FREE COUNTRY, RIGHT? I choose my clothes (sixties retro), I choose my shoes (Nikes), I choose my CDs (Hendrix and Nine Inch Nails), I choose my friends (you know who you are). If I were an adult (which I'm not – I'm a fourteen-year-old eighth-grade girl named Sun) I could vote, could choose my car, my career, whatever – like I said, a free country, right?

Wrong.

Quiz time: Please take out a number two lead pencil; *do not* open the test booklet until you're told. Seriously, my question to you is this: What's the most majorly thing in your life that you *can't* choose? The answer is as simple as the eyes and nose on your face: your parents. Your parents and your brothers or sisters. That's because no matter how free you think you are, the one thing nobody can choose for herself is her own family.

Here's another way of putting it: Being born is something like arriving at a restaurant where there are no waitrons and no menus. Your table is set and your food is there waiting for you. It might be fresh shrimp, it might be steak, it might be macaroni hot dish, it might be all broccoli; for some kids there might be no food at all, maybe not even a table.

Me? I was fairly lucky. My parents are (1) there, and (2) at least semicool most of the time. My dad's an accountant and my mom's a college professor. Both are in their middle forties, physically fit, and usually unembarrassing in public. My gripe is the old basic one for girls: My father spends way more time on sports with my brother, Luke, than with me.

Luke is in sixth grade, is already taller than me, and can pound me at basketball. At Ping-Pong. At any sport. You name it, he crushes me. I want to say right here I'm not a klutz. I'm nearly five feet six and have at least average coordination; on our basketball team I'm third off the bench, which is not that shabby considering that our school, Hawk Bend, is a basketball power in central Minnesota. But I won't play one-on-one with Luke anymore. No way. Who likes to lose every time? It's not like he's mean or wants to humiliate me – he's actually pretty decent for a twerpy sixth-grade boy – it's just that he's a natural athlete and I'm not.

I am thinking these thoughts as I sit next to my parents watching Luke's team play Wheatville. Luke just made a nifty spin move (of course, he's the starting point guard) and drove the lane for a layup. My mother, who comes to most games, stares at Luke with her usual astounded look. She murmurs to my father, who comes to all our games, "How did he *do* that?"

"Head fake right, plant pivot foot, big swing with leading leg, and bingo – he's by," my dad whispers. A quiet but intense man with salt-and-pepper hair, he speaks from the side of his mouth, for there are always parents of other sixth-graders nearby.

"He amazes me," my mother says. She has not taken her eyes off Luke. I hate to agree, but she's right – all of which clouds further my normally "sunny" disposition. I remember Dad and Luke working last winter on that very move in the basement; I went downstairs to see what was going on, and they both looked up at me like I was an alien from the *Weekly World News*. My father soon enough bounced the ball to me, and I gave it a try, but I could never get my spin dribble to rotate quickly enough and in a straight line forward to the basket. Not like you-know-who. "Watch Luke," my father said. "He'll demonstrate."

Now, at least it's the third quarter of the game and Luke

already has a lot of points and his team is ahead by twenty so the coach will take him out soon – though not quite soon enough for Wheatville, or me. At the other end of the court Luke's loose, skinny-legged body and flopping yellow hair darts forward like a stroke of heat lightning to deflect the ball.

"Go, Luke!" my father says, half rising from his seat.

Luke is already gone, gathering up the ball on a breakaway, finishing with a soft layup high off the board. People clap wildly.

I clap slowly. Briefly. Politely. My mother just shakes her head. "How does he *do* that?"

"Ask *him*," I mutter.

"Pardon, Sun?" my mom says abstractedly.

"Nothing." I check the scoreboard, then my own watch. I've seen enough. Below, at floor level, some friends are passing. "I think I'll go hang with Tara and Rochelle," I say to my parents.

"Sure," my mother says vacantly.

Dad doesn't hear me or see me leave.

As I clump down the bleachers there is more cheering, but I prefer not to look. "Sun." What a stupid name – and by the way I do not *ever* answer to "Sunny". I was allegedly born on a Sunday, on a day when the sun was particularly bright, or so my parents maintain. I seriously doubt their version (someday I'm going to look up the actual weather report on March 18, 1980). I'm sure it was a Monday; either that or I was switched at the hospital. Or maybe it was Luke – one of us, definitely, was switched.

Rochelle, actually looking once or twice at the game, says right off, "Say, wasn't that your little brother?"

"I have no brother," I mutter. "He's a smooth little dude," Tara says, glancing over her shoulder. "Kinda cute, actually."

"Can I have some popcorn or what?" I say.

"Or what," Rochelle says, covering her bag.

They giggle hysterically. Real comediennes, these two.

"When's your next game?" Tara says to me, relenting, giving me three whole kernels.

"The last one is Tuesday night," I answer. "A make-up game with Big Falls."

58

"Here or away?"

"Here."

"With your record, maybe you could get your little brother to play for your team."

"Yeah – a little eye shadow, a training bra," adds Rochelle, "everyone would think he was you!"

I growl something unprintable to my friends and go buy my own bag of popcorn.

At supper that night Luke and I stare at each other during grace, our usual game – see who will blink first. Tonight it is me. I glare down at my broccoli and fish; I can feel him grinning.

"And thank you, God, for bouncing the ball our way once again," my father finishes. "Amen." If God doesn't understand sports metaphors, our family is in huge trouble.

"Well," my father says, looking at Luke expectantly.

"A deep subject," Luke says automatically, reaching for his milk, automatically.

Both of them are trying not to be the first one to talk about the game.

"How was your day, Sun?" my mother says.

"I hate it when you do that."

"Do what?" my mother says.

"It's condescending," I add.

"What is condescending?" she protests.

"Asking me about my day when the thing on everybody's mind is Luke's usual great game. Why not just say it: 'So, Luke, what were the numbers?'"

There is silence; I see Luke cast an uncertain glance towards my father.

"That's not at all what I meant," Mother says.

"And watch that tone of voice," my father warns me.

"So how many points *did* you get?" I say to Luke, clanking the broccoli spoon back into the dish, holding the dish in front of his face; he hates broccoli.

He shrugs, mumbles, "Not sure, really."

"How many?" I press.

59

"I dunno. Fifteen or so." But he can't help himself. He bites his lip, tries to scowl, fakes a cough, but the smile is too strong.

"How *many*?" I demand.

"Maybe it was twenty," he murmurs.

I pick up a large clump of broccoli and aim it at his head.

"Sun!" my father exclaims.

Luke's eyes widen. "Twenty-six!" he squeaks.

"There. That wasn't so difficult, was it?" I say, biting the head off the broccoli.

Luke lets out a breath, begins to eat. There is a silence for a while.

"By the way – nice steal there at the end," I say to him as I pass the fish to Father.

Luke looks up at me from the top of his eyes. "Thanks," he says warily.

"It's something I should work on," I add.

"I'll help you!" Luke says instantly and sincerely. "Right after supper!"

At this syrupy sibling exchange, my parents relax and dinner proceeds smoothly.

Later, during dessert, when my father and Luke have finally debriefed themselves – quarter by quarter, play by play – on the game, I wait for Dad's usual "Well, who's next on the schedule, Luke?" He doesn't disappoint me.

"Clearville, I think," Luke says.

"Any breakdown on them? Stats?"

"They're eight-four on the season, have that big centre who puts up *numbers*, plus a smooth point guard. They beat us by six last time," Luke says. My mind skips ahead twenty years and sees Luke with his own accounting office, crunching tax returns by day and shooting hoops long into the evening.

"Big game, then, yes?" my father remarks, his fingers beginning to drum on the table. "You'll have to box out – keep that big guy off the boards. And if their point guard penetrates, collapse inside – make him prove he can hit the jumper."

"He can't hit no jumpers," Luke says through a large bite of cake. "He shoots bricks, and I'm going to shut him down like a bike lock."

"Huh?" I say.

"What?" Luke says. "What'd I say now?"

"First off, it's 'any jumpers'. And second, how do you shut someone down 'like a bike lock'?"

"Actually, it's not a bad simile," my mother says. "If this fellow is 'smooth', so, in a way, is a bicycle – the way it rolls and turns – and a bike lock, well . . ." She trails off, looking at me.

I shrug and stare down at my fish. It has not been a good day for either of us.

"And who does *your* team play next, Sun?" my father asks dutifully.

"Big Falls. Tuesday night," I say, I look up and watch his face carefully.

"Tuesday night, isn't that . . ." he begins.

"I'm afraid I'll miss it, honey," my mother interjects. "I have that teachers' education conference in Minneapolis, remember?"

"Sure, Mom, no problem." I keep my eyes on my father; on Luke, who's thinking. I am waiting for the light-bulb (twenty watts, maximum) to go on in his brain.

"Hey – Tuesday night is my game, too," Luke says suddenly.

"Yes, I thought so," my father murmurs. The one-on-one experts have finally put two and two together.

"What time are your games?" my mother asks.

"Seven," Luke and I say simultaneously.

My father looks to me, then to Luke. He's frowning. Suddenly his gaze lightens. "By any chance are they both at the high school? In the adjoining gyms?"

"Middle school," Luke says.

"High school," I follow.

"Damn," my father says, "they ought to take whoever schedules sporting events in this school system and—"

"I'm sure it couldn't be helped, dear," my mother interjects. "Sun's is a make-up game, after all."

"And the last one of the season," I add.

My father looks to Luke. "So is yours, right? The last one of the season?"

61

Luke nods. He and I look at each other. I smile. I love moral dilemmas, especially when they're not mine.

My father turns to my mother.

"Sorry," she says to him, "I'm delivering a speech in Minneapolis. There's no way I can miss it."

"Well," my father says, drumming his fingers, "I'll have to think this one through."

Amazingly, Luke keeps his promise, and after dinner we work on stealing. It is chilly outside in March, with patches of leftover snowbanks along the north side of the garage (this is Minnesota, remember), but the asphalt is clear.

"There are two main types of steals," Luke says, dribbling. "First is the most basic, 'the unprotected ball'. As your man is dribbling, he is not shielding the ball with his body, and so you go for it."

"I have part of a brain," I say, and lunge for the deflection – but Luke instantly back-dribbles, and I miss.

"It's all in the timing," he says, "all in when you start your move. Don't start when the ball is coming back up to my hand – begin your move just when the ball *leaves* my hand, just when it's released and heading downward."

I track him, waiting – then try it. This time I actually knock the ball away.

"See?" Luke says. "That gives you the maximum time for your reach-in."

We practice this a few more times.

"Be sure to reach with your outside hand," Luke cautions, "or else you might get called for a reach-in foul."

We keep working for quite a while. I start to get every third one, but I'm still not very good at it.

"It's coming," Luke says, then holds the ball. I kick away a pebble, which clatters against the garage door.

"The second type of steal is called the wraparound. It's when your man is dribbling and you reach way around behind, almost wrapping your arm around him, and knock the ball away." He flips me the ball, has me dribble, and snakes loose the ball two out of three times. Then he takes the ball back, and we work on this one for a while. I get one out of ten at best. Soon I am panting.

"The wraparound is the toughest one," Luke says. "Maybe you need longer arms or something."

From the window, my father is watching us. "Again," I say crabbily to Luke. Soon I am stumbling-tired and getting no wraparound deflections or steals at all.

"Hey – it'll come," Luke says, bouncing the ball to me. I slam the ball hard onto the cold asphalt and back into my hands.

"Yeah. Like in 2010 maybe," I say, then mutter something unprintable.

"Ah . . . I think I'll go have some more cake," Luke says.

"Fine!" I bark. He heads off.

"By the way," I call after him, "who taught you those stealing moves?" The middle-school coaches teach both the girls' and the boys' teams, and I am always on the lookout for coaches who treat boys and girls differently. Nothing ticks me off more than that.

"Who taught me? Coach Dad," Luke says with an innocent smile.

I don't smile. I glare at Luke, then to the window, which is empty.

"What?" Luke says, glancing behind. "What did I say now?"

"Nothing." I turn away, take the ball, and begin to bank hard shots off the backboard, none of which fall.

That night, as my father sits at the kitchen table rattling his calculator keys and turning the pages of someone's tax return (from March through April 15 we leave him alone), I find myself rattling the dishes hard and loud as I clean up the kitchen.

"Was there something? . . ." he says irritatedly, glancing up only briefly from his papers.

"No," I say, and stomp past him upstairs to my room.

Later I hear my mother speaking softly to my father. He lets out a sigh and pushes back from the table. Soon I hear his footsteps on the stairs, and then he pops his head partway into my room, where I am reading. "Everything OK, Sun?"

"Sure," I mutter.

"Sure sure?"

I shrug.

He leans in my doorway. "So what is it?" he asks, checking his watch.

"How come you taught Luke those two types of steals and not me?" I turn to him. My eyes, disgustingly, feel glassy and spilly; they are about to dump water down my cheeks.

He stares. "Steals? Oh, you mean . . . Yes, well . . ." He trails off and stares at some empty space in front of him, thinking. Then he turns to me. "I guess I just naturally do more sports stuff with Luke because we're both boys – I mean I once was, and he's one now, that sort of thing," he finishes lamely.

"Well, I play basketball, too, dammit!" I say. I try to be hard-boiled but a large tear rolls down my cheek. "Damn," I blurt, and start crying for real.

He stares at me, then moves imperceptibly, as if to come forward either to smack me for swearing or to take me in his arms. But accountants are accountants because most of them are not good with other things – like feelings. With a confused look on his face, my father retreats from my room.

In the morning when I wake up, there is a note taped to my door. In his small, careful handwriting my father has written, "Dear Sun: There is a third type of steal . . ."

That Saturday, when Luke is gone to hockey, my father appears in the TV room wearing his tennis shoes and sweats. "'Stealing for Girls', a sports clinic by yours truly, begins in fifteen minutes, garage-side."

I smile, grab the remote, and shoot the TV dead.

Before we go outside, my father sits at the kitchen table and begins drawing neat X's and O's on graph paper. "We'll call this third type the prediction pass steal. It's something that works best with a zone defence."

"OK," I say. On my team we have been learning the zone, and zone traps, though we haven't used them much.

"A half-court zone defence forces the team on offence to work the ball around the perimeter."

I nod as he draws lines in a large circle.

"The faster the ball movement, the tougher it is for the defence to shift accordingly."

I nod. I know all this.

"The offensive point guard will sooner or later get into what you might call the automatic pass mode – he receives a pass from, say, his right side, and automatically turns to pass to his left."

"Yeah, sure," I murmur, for I am thinking of something that has always puzzled me.

"What is it?" my father asks with a trace of impatience.

"If you never played basketball in high school or college, how come you know so much about the game?"

He looks up straight at me. There is a long moment of silence. "I would like to have played," he says simply, "but it was a big school."

I meet his gaze, then put my hand on his shoulder.

He smiles, a small but real smile, and we both turn back to the graph paper.

"Anyway, when the point guard gets sloppy," he continues, "that's when the smart defensive man can start to think about a prediction pass steal."

"The defensive point guard?"

"No," my father says immediately. "The offensive point guard is used to that; he's been conditioned to watch out for that kind of steal. What he's not expecting is the weak-side defensive guard or even the forward to break up and across, slanting through the lane towards the key and picking off the pass. A lot of the quick but small college teams use it."

"Show me," I say, staring down at the paper.

He grabs a fresh graph. "Imagine a basic zone defence that's shifting to the ball."

I close my eyes. "Got it," I say.

"If the offence is moving the ball sharply, the defensive point guard has the toughest job. He usually can't keep up with the ball movement."

I nod. I keep my eyes closed.

"So the passes out front become 'gimmes'; they're not contested."

I nod again.

"And after a while, the offensive point guard gets sloppy. That's when one of the defensive players down low – the forward or centre – can make his move. He flashes all the way up, comes out of nowhere for the steal."

My smile opens my eyes.

"Keep in mind it will only work once or twice," my father cautions, "and the timing has to be perfect – or the defence will get burned."

I look down to his drawing, see the open hole left by the steal attempt.

"Burned bad," he adds. "But if it works – bingo – he's gone for an easy layup."

I correct him: "*She's* gone."

Outside, for want of five offensive players, my father presses into service a sawhorse, three garbage cans, and my mother. "I just love my team," she says wryly.

"This won't take long," my dad says. Mom shivers; the weather is cloudy, with rain forecast.

"Sun, you're the weak-side defensive guard," he directs. I position myself, back to the basket. "Honey, you're our offensive point guard," he says to my mother.

"I've never been a point guard; I've never been a guard of any kind," she protests.

"First time for everything," my dad retorts.

Actually, I can tell that they're both having at least a little fun.

"Now," he says to my mom, "imagine you have just received a pass from the sawhorse, and in turn you'll be passing to me."

My mother, the orange ball looking very large in her hands, says, "Thanks – sawhorse," and turns and passes to my dad.

"Now – Sun!" he calls, but I break up way too late.

"Again," my father says.

This time I break up too soon, and my mother stops her pass.

"Again," my father says.

66

I trot back to my position and try it again. On the sixth try I time it perfectly: I catch her pass chest-high and am gone for an imaginary layup.

"Excellent!" my father calls. "Again."

We practise until we are glowing in the chilly March morning, until an icy rain starts spattering down and the ball becomes too slick to hold.

Afterwards, we are sitting at the kitchen table drinking hot chocolate when outside a car door slams – Luke's ride – and then Luke thumps into the house. "Hey," he says, pointing over his shoulder, "what's with the garbage cans and the sawhorse?"

The three of us look at each other; I smile and say nothing.

For the next several days, my father and I work exactly forty-five minutes per evening on the prediction pass steal. I let Luke join us only because we need another passer. The weather remains lousy, and my mother freezes her butt off, and Luke complains about not getting to try the prediction steal himself, but my father ignores all that. He is too busy fine-tuning my timing, my breakaways.

And, suddenly, it is Tuesday morning of game day.

Both games.

"Huge day – two big games," my father says, first thing, at breakfast. He drums his fingers, glances at his briefcase, at the clock.

Luke glares at me. He is not happy about this week and his role as perpetual passer. "I guess I know which game *you're* going to," he mutters to my father.

My father says nothing.

Warming up with the team, I have the usual butterflies. The Big Falls girls look like their name – big, with huge hair tied back and bouncing like waterfalls as they do their layups. I try not to look at them, but can't help but hear their chatter, the chirp and thud of their shoes. Even their feet are huge.

I look around the gym. No family. No Dad. I miss my layup.

Just before tip-off, from my spot on the bench, I look around one last time. No family. No father. I sigh and try to focus on the game.

Which is going to be a tough one all the way. The teams are well matched at every position, and we trade basket for basket – bad news for me. I ride the pine all the way through the first quarter.

We do our "Hawk Bend Fliers!" send-off whoop to start the second quarter, and as I head back to the bench I scan the small crowd. Still no father. But it's just as well, I think gloomily as I settle onto the bench – at least at Luke's game he's seeing Luke play. Logically, if I were a parent I wouldn't come to my game, either.

Watching, chin in hands, that second quarter, with a sparse, quiet crowd giving neither team much support, I begin to think dark but true thoughts: that really, in the end, each of us is alone. That each of us, by what we choose to do, is responsible for what we achieve and how we feel about ourselves. That each of us—

"Sun, Sun!" An elbow, Jenny's, jabs me in the ribs: the coach is calling for me.

"Sun; check in for Rachel," Coach Brown says, then adds, "At forward," giving me a fleeting, get-your-head-in-the-game glance.

I have to ask Rachel who she's guarding. Tired, irritated at having to pause on her way off the floor, she looks around and finally points to a hefty, five-foot-ten forward with major pimples on her shoulders and neck. I trot up close.

"What are you staring at?" The sweaty Big Falls forward says straight off. Then she leans close to me and glares.

"There's a new soap that might clear those up," I say, letting my eyes fall to her neck and shoulders.

"Listen, you little—" she says, but the horn drowns out the rest.

Then the ball is in play. It comes quickly to my man, who puts her shoulder down and drives the lane. I keep my feet planted and draw the charging foul.

"Way to go, Sun," my team calls as we head up the floor, and my mood lightens considerably.

In my two minutes of play I make one lucky basket and draw one foul – a reach-in steal attempt. I try to remember that timing is everything. I also see that our team is quicker, but Big Falls is

69

stronger inside. Pimple Shoulders muscles me out of the way for an easy bank shot, like I was a mosquito on an alligator's back. She outweighs me by eighty pounds, minimum.

At the next time-out Rachel comes back in and I end up sitting next to the coach. I watch us get beat inside by some teeth-jarring picks and back screens; the score gradually tilts in favour of Big Falls. At the half we are down 28–21.

In the locker room the first five players lie red-faced and flat on their backs on the benches. "They're shoving underneath," Rachel complains.

"No – they're outmuscling us," Coach retorts. "Position! We've got to get position and stay planted. Like Sun did right away when she came in – get planted and draw the foul."

I play it very cool and do not change expressions.

The coach heads to the chalkboard and begins to draw X's and O's. "They might be big, but they're slow. In the third quarter I want us to run, run, run – fast-break them until their butts are dragging."

"Or ours," Rachel mutters.

"You don't want to play hard, we've got people who do!" Coach barks.

Rachel zips her lips, stares at the ceiling.

During the half-time shoot I scan the crowd. Still nobody. I feel something inside me harden further, and centre itself; it's a flash of what life will be like when I go away to college, when I'll truly be on my own. Just me. No family whatsoever. Just me shlumping along through life.

On the bench as the third quarter begins, for some reason I finally get focused. I sit next to the coach; I chatter out encouragement. Our fast break begins to work. After they score or we get a rebound, Rachel rips the ball to one side or the other while Jenny, our point guard, breaks up the centre. She takes the pass at the half-court line, then does her thing – either driving the lane or dishing off to the trailers. We miss some easy layups but still pull within one point.

Big Falls calls time-out. Our subs are ecstatic, but the starting five stand bent over, hands on knees, wheezing.

"Let's try to keep the fast break working through the end of this quarter," Coach Brown says, "and then we'll figure out something else."

Our starters manage a weak "Go Fliers" and trudge back onto the floor.

In the final two minutes of the third quarter I watch as Big Falls shuts down the fast break like . . . like a bicycle lock. Simple, really – just some pressure on the out-of-bounds first pass, plus coverage on the sides – and we do not score again. But I have been watching them on offence. Nearly every time down the court, Pimple Shoulders rears up inside, then looks for the pass from the point guard – who has taken very few shots from the perimeter, including zero three-point attempts.

"Zone," I say to myself. "In the fourth quarter we should go zone."

Coach Brown looks at me. Then back to the action. He strokes his chin.

At the final quarter break he kneels on the floor. "Take a load off," he commands, and the starting five slump into chairs. He points, one by one, to the next five, and we check in. Back in the huddle, Coach Brown has drawn some scrawling maps of X's and O's. "Zone defence," he says, with a wink to me. "Let's collapse inside and make them shoot from the perimeter. Make them prove they can hit the jumpers. But box out and get that rebound," he adds. "We've got to have the ball to score."

We fire up and trot on to the floor. For some reason I look to the middle of the bleachers – and see my father. His briefcase rests beside him and his grey suit coat is folded neatly over it.

"Zone! Box and one!" the Big Falls point guard calls out immediately, and begin to move the ball crisply side to front to side. It's clear they've had a zone thrown at them before. Still bench-stiff, we have trouble keeping up with the passes, and their point guard takes an uncontested shot from within the key – but bricks it. Wendy rips off the rebound and we move the ball cautiously upcourt. Our second-team guards have no future with the Harlem Globetrotters in terms of ballhandling, but we do know how to pick-and-roll.

I fake to the baseline, then break up and set a screen for Shanna. She rubs off her girl – who hits me, blindside, hard – as I roll to the inside. I'm looking for the ball, and suddenly, thanks to a nifty bounce pass, it's right at my chest. I clamp on it, take one dribble, brace for a hammer blow from Pimple Shoulders, and go up for the lay-in. I feel the oncoming air rush of a large-body (the image of a 747 jetliner on a crash course with a seagull flashes through my mind) but I don't alter my flight path. The ball feels good off my fingertips. As my feet touch down and I open my eyes, the ball is settling through the net and Pimple Shoulders is skidding along the hardwood runway and there is major cheering from our bench. Me? I am just happy to be heading upcourt with all my feathers intact.

The Big Falls outside shooting continues to bang hard off the rim, and we continue to box out and get the rebound play and score on basic pick-and-rolls. We go up 42–38, and our bench is screaming and bouncing up and down in their chairs.

But Big Falls get smart: They throw a zone defence at us. Not great passers, and worse outside shooters, we turn the ball over three times; barely fifty seconds later, Big Falls is up by two, 44–42, and Coach Brown is screaming for a time-out. By the time the ref stops the clock there is less than three minutes left in the game.

"OK, good job, second team," he calls, pointing for the first team to check back in. "Stay with the zone defence, but let's run the fast break."

We all clap once, together, and send the starters back on to the floor.

"Nice work out there," the coach says to me, and motions for me to sit by him. "Stay ready."

The first team, refreshed, runs a fast break for a quick bucket and knots the score at 44–all. The teams trade baskets, then settle into solid defence, and suddenly there is less than one minute to play. Both the score and my gut are knotted. The Big Falls point guard launches a three-pointer, which goes through, but we come back with a fast break on which Rachel does some kind of wild, falling, 180-degree, dipsy-do finger-roll shot – which falls! We are down by one point, but Rachel is down, too, with a turned ankle. There are thirty seconds left.

We help her off the court. Done for the day, she cries with pain and anger.

"Sun – check in and go to forward," the coach says.

As I pause at the scorer's table, everything seems exaggeratedly clear, as if magnified: the black and white zebra stripes of the officials, the seams of the yellow wood floor, the orange rim worn to bare, shiny metal on the inside. I stare at the ball the ref is holding and can imagine its warm, tight sphere in my hands. I want that ball. For the first time in my basketball career I want the ball, bad.

The Big Falls girls are slapping high fives like the game is over; after all, they have possession with a one-point lead. The ref calls time-in, and Big Falls bounces the ball inbounds handily and pushes it quickly up the floor. There they spread the offence and begin to work the ball around the perimeter: side to front to side to front. It's too early for us to foul, so we stay with our zone defence. Their point guard, still jazzed from making the three-point basket, is loose and smart-mouthed. As she receives the ball she automatically passes it to the opposite side.

Which is when I suddenly see not Big Falls players but garbage cans and a sawhorse. To the side, on the bench, I see Coach Brown rising to signal it's time to foul, but I have been counting off another kind of time: the Big Falls passing rhythm. On the far side, away from the ball, when orange is flashing halfway to the point guard, I begin my break. Smart Mouth receives the ball, turns, and passes it. Her eyes bug out as I arrow into view; she tries to halt her pass but it's too late. I catch the ball and am gone. There is only open floor in front and sudden cheering from the sides, and, overly excited, I launch my layup at about the free throw line – but the ball goes in anyway. The Hawk Bend crowd goes crazy.

Down by one point, Big Falls calls a frantic time-out at the five-second mark. Our players are delirious, but Coach Brown is not. "Watch for the long pass, the long pass!" he rants. "They have a set play. Don't foul – especially on the three-point shot."

But we're only eighth-graders; at times we don't listen well.

Sure enough, Big Falls screens on the inbound pass, which Pimple Shoulders fires full court. There the point guard takes an off-balance shot – and is fouled by Shanna as time runs out.

Shanna looks paralysed. She can't believe she did it.

"Three-point attempt – three foul shots!" the ref calls.

We clear off the free throw line and watch her make the first two – to tie – and miss the third. The game goes into overtime.

Back in the huddle we try to get pumped again, but I can tell it's not going to happen. We are stunned and flat. We lose in overtime by four points.

Back home we have a late supper: broccoli, fish sticks, and rice. I stare at my plate as my father finishes grace. Then he looks up. "Well," he says.

"A very deep subject," Luke replies, grabbing the bread. His team won, of course, by twenty-six points.

I just sit there, slumped and staring.

"You should have seen it," my father begins, speaking to Luke. "We're down by one and your sister is low on the weak side. The Big Falls point guard is not paying attention . . ." Slowly I look up. I listen as my father tells the story of my one and only career steal. He re-creates it so well that Luke stops eating and his mouth drops open slightly. "Rad!" Luke says at the finish, then asks me more about my game. I shrug, but end up giving him a virtual play-by-play of the last two minutes.

When I'm done, Luke lets out a breath and looks squarely at me. "Wow – I wish I could have been there!"

I stop to stare at him.

"What – what'd I say?" Luke says warily.

I just smile, and pass my little brother the broccoli.

WET BOB, DRY BOB

JOHN BRANFIELD

H E BUMPED DOWN THE STONY TRACK, braking hard, until he came to the beach. Although he was late, he paused for a moment, hands held on top of the dropped handlebars, one foot on the ground and his bike slewed at an angle beneath him. He looked across the water. Some two dozen red sails were moving in all directions. Further out to sea a line of white sails spread along the horizon, all of them heeling over on the same tack.

There was only one sail on the beach, the red sail of his father's dinghy. It flapped on the mast and made a slapping noise as the boom swung from side to side. He sat and watched while his dad tried to launch the boat, pushing the trolley ahead of him down the beach in the off-shore wind. He was putting an enormous effort into it, holding up the trolley with one hand and pushing on the bows with the other, leaning forward and digging his feet into the gravel and stones, splaying them out to get more hold. He wore old shoes that he had cut the toes out of, so that the water ran out of them – "self-drainers", he called them – and a pair of shorts. In his yellow life-jacket and with his thin arms and legs, he looked like a giant insect.

One of the wheels of the trolley stuck against a pebble.

His father put his head down and heaved all the more. When the boat would not shift, he straightened up. The boy watched as he tried to lift the pebble aside. His dad bent over it, grasping it with both hands. His backside stuck up into the air. The boy felt a sudden impulse to give it a kick and send his father sprawling face-first into the water. He shifted uneasily on his saddle, surprised by the strength of the feeling.

The pebble sucked up out of the sand, and his father cast it away. As he turned, he looked up the beach and saw the boy sitting on his bicycle.

"Come on, David," he shouted. "Give me a hand."

His face was bright red, though perhaps it was a reflection of the sail. He held out his wrist and pointed at his watch in large pantomime gestures, as though he thought his voice would not carry across the shore.

"Hurry up," he yelled.

Then he lifted the trolley again and started to push, still with a touch of over-acting in his movements.

Dave left his bike at the back of the clubhouse and ran across the beach, feeling guilty at having stayed so long watching his father struggling on his own. He pushed on one side of the boat, and it rolled down to the edge of the water.

"We'll never make it," said his dad. He glanced at his watch again. "Three minutes to go."

The other dinghies were all huddled behind the starting line, looking as though they were sailing into and over each other as they tried to get into a good position to be first away.

"I'm sorry," said Dave.

His dad held the boat into the wind. Dave picked up the trolley and ran up the beach with it. When he came back his father was attaching the rudder, getting soaked to the waist.

"Come on, get aboard," he shouted.

Dave scrambled in over the bows and his dad turned the boat. The boom swung to the side, the sail filled and the dinghy started to move away from the shore. His dad, in danger of being left behind, flung himself over the side, the boat tilted with his weight, and Dave leaned out on the other side to

76

keep it balanced. His father hauled himself in, like a wet fish coming aboard, grasped the tiller and tried to untangle himself from the sheet, which was wound around his legs. It was not a very dignified departure for the secretary of the sailing club.

Dave hoisted the foresail, cleating down the halyard. He passed the foresail sheet through the fairlead and held on to the end. There was no air behind the mainsail, and the foresail was not drawing at all; he passed it out on the other side so that they could goose-wing to the starting line. He had time to put on his life-jacket.

His dad too had sorted out the mainsheet after the rush of setting sail.

"Where on earth did you get to?" he asked crossly. "I thought you reckoned you were as fast as the car on that bike of yours."

It was true, or very nearly. He always helped his dad to pack the car with the boating gear, then left on his bicycle just before him and he was usually more than halfway to the sailing club before his father caught up. He always helped to put the boat in the water.

"I tried a different way," said Dave.

"It must have been a long short-cut."

"It was."

In fact, when he had reached the bypass around the town he had looked over the parapet of the bridge and seen the dual carriageway stretching away into the distance. It was almost empty of traffic. The temptation had been too great. He had swung into the slip road and belted down the slope to get up as much speed as possible. He was really motoring when he joined the bypass.

And once he was on it, there was no way of turning back until he reached the roundabout at the far end, five miles away. He supposed he could have carried his bike across the central reservation, and turned back. But he did not even think about it. The speed was exhilarating. He passed the junction and kept going. He circled the roundabout, and came back along the other side of the dual carriageway, the wind against him.

It was a ten-mile detour. No wonder his dad had got to the beach before him.

"Half a minute to go," said his father. He pumped the tiller, in a useless attempt to get the boat to go faster.

They were a good two hundred metres away. One boat crossed the line, turned and came up to it again. The starting gun went and the other boats leaped forward past the marker buoy. Three minutes later David and his father in *Happy Days* crossed over and started trying to catch up the others.

They were sailing for the first buoy, with the wind on their starboard quarter. Mr Robinson had pulled in the mainsail a little tighter, and Dave had returned the foresail to the port side. The sails were drawing well, and the water slapped and gurgled along the sides.

"A good start is half the battle," said his father. "Nigel always liked a good start."

"Mm," said Dave.

"We haven't got a chance now."

Dave knew it was his fault.

His father sat comfortably in the stern. "I hope Nigel got off well," he said.

"I expect so," said David. He knew that his brother was spending the weekend on a cross-channel race. They had left at eight-thirty last evening, to sail through the night.

"With this wind they'll be in Cherbourg by now," said his dad. "They'll be having cocktails aboard the *Gloriana*. She's a Swan 65. Nigel says her sheet winches are the size of dustbins."

He glanced up at the tell-tale on the stay.

"The size of dustbins," he repeated, very amused by the expression. Then, "Good old Nigel," he added.

Good old Nigel, thought David.

"Watch that boat in front," ordered his dad. "Let me know when she goes round the buoy."

Dave twisted into position to look under the boom.

"Now!" he said.

Mr Robinson looked at his watch. "We can see if we've gained anything by the time we go round."

But when they reached the buoy they were still three minutes behind.

They were sailing with the wind on their port beam. There was not much for Dave to do. He began to feel cold and cramped. He wanted to move, to exert himself more. He thought of his ride along the bypass.

And then the wind, which had been quite fresh all day, began to drop. His dad looked puzzled; he turned his cheek to the breeze. "Hello," he said.

To make it worse, the wind seemed to drop only around them. Way ahead, the rest of the fleet was sailing merrily on. The leader had already rounded the next buoy, and was now tacking into the wind, forging into the waves, its sail bobbing to and fro.

The boat ahead was drawing farther away. Dave could see the cat's-paws of wind on the water around it, while the sea around *Happy Days* had turned as smooth as glass. He could see the weed in the water. The sail flapped idly.

The dinghy glided a little farther, and then lost all way. It was just a piece of flotsam on the sea, drifting with the tide.

Dave felt guilty, as though the failure of the wind was his fault too. If he hadn't gone bombing down the bypass, they would have been in at the start and still have had a wind. He looked up the mast to the racing burgee at the top, a little square of red nylon, quite still against the blue sky and white clouds.

When he was younger, it used to thrill him to be on the boat. He used to be as keen as Nigel. But now as they wallowed in the calm he admitted to himself something that he had never admitted before.

I hate sailing, he thought. It was boring being crew for his dad. He never wanted to sail with him again.

"There's nothing for it," said Mr Robinson. "We'll just have to whistle for a wind."

And he started to whistle, gratingly, as he had always done. Dave wondered how he could tell him.

The cycling club in the town behind the bypass met on Thursday evenings in the church hall. He went along for the first time, and felt a bit strange. A boy and a girl were playing table-tennis, and other people were sitting around drinking coffee and talking bikes. Two men in their twenties were discussing frames, the merits of alloy or titanium. Dave could not really follow the conversation, with all the talk of Reynolds five-three-one and Reynolds seven-five-three, Campags, Cinellis and Condors.

A man called Harry told him about the club, the time-trials they held each Friday evening and the club run each Sunday, meeting at ten o'clock outside the Leisure Centre.

Only this Sunday there would be no run, as the club was holding its annual Kermess.

"You ought to enter the schoolboys' event," he said.

"I don't think my bike's up to it." He did not have a handbuilt frame, or Campagnolo gears.

"Let's have a look."

They went outside to where his bicycle was leaning against the churchyard wall. It was a Viscount, with a black frame and silver trim, black mudguards and a black suede saddle, worn rather smooth in places. It had heavy pedals with reflectors on them. It seemed too heavy altogether for racing.

Harry looked it over carefully.

"It's all right," he said. "If you take up cycling there are some changes you could make. You could get some quick-release sprint wheels and change to tubs instead of tyres. But this will do fine to begin with. Why don't you come along tomorrow evening and get yourself timed over five miles? Then if you do well, you can enter the race on Sunday."

They met for the time-trials at a road junction halfway along the bypass, where the main road passed beneath the dual carriageway and a slip road linked the two.

Dave arrived early, but there were already half a dozen people there, changing out of cycling bottoms and track suits into cycling jerseys and shorts. Dave wore the same shorts that he wore for sailing, and he was a bit self-conscious about them.

Everyone else had cycling shorts in shiny black material that fitted close to the thighs, with chamois-leather seats. They talked about the weather and their best times.

A boy from the same year at school came up to him. He looked the part, in a long yellow jersey and black shorts; his lightweight bike was gold and black to match.

"Start a minute before me," he said. "Then you can try to keep ahead."

They gave their names and kept together in the line-up. About a dozen other people had arrived. Harry started the clock. There was a count-down to one minute, and then the first rider was off.

Some of the riders had watches clamped to their handlebars. Another boy was rubbing oil over his legs; it smelt of coconut.

After three minutes Dave went to the start. One of the club members held him upright on his bike, and Harry started the count-down. Dave went up the slope and on to the bypass.

He did not try to pace himself, he went as hard as he could all the way. Before he was halfway to the roundabout, the boy in black and yellow sailed past him. He increased his effort to keep up with him, but soon fell behind.

At the roundabout a club official waved him on. Soon there was a smell of coconut in the air, and then the boy with the oiled legs whizzed by. By now Black-and-Gold was a small dot way down the carriageway.

He reached the junction and sped down the slip road past the time-keepers. He felt he was slower than a week ago, on his way to the beach. He sat down on the verge to recover his breath.

Harry came through the underpass. "How did you get on?" he asked.

He went to the time-keeper and got his time. Sixteen minutes, twenty-three seconds.

"That's not bad," said Harry. "It's worth entering the schoolboys' event on Sunday."

They had always, as long as he could remember, at first with Nigel and later without him, spent Sunday afternoons in summer at the sailing-club. Mr Robinson after all was honorary secretary; he needed to be available. Mrs Robinson made the sandwiches for the club teas. They did not always sail, but they always had their tea on the terrace, or in the clubhouse if it was wet.

"I've entered a cycle race," he said, as soon as he got home from the time-trials.

"Yes," said his mum.

"The cycling club are having their Kermess."

"Kermess?" repeated his dad. "What's a Kermess?"

"It's like a regatta," said his mum. "Only it's cycle races instead of boats."

"Where is it?"

"On the industrial estate."

"Hm," said his dad. "When?"

"On Sunday."

"But it's the Commodore's Cup on Sunday."

There was an awkward silence.

"You could get someone else to crew," said his mum. "There are always plenty of boys around the club looking for a race."

"It's not the same," said Mr Robinson. "When Nigel was David's age, we won the cup for the first time, and held it for three years. I'd hoped this year we'd win it back."

"I'm sorry," said Dave.

"I've nothing against cycling," said his dad, after a while. "But I don't understand how anyone can prefer to spend the afternoon cycling round and round an industrial estate, with his head bent over a pair of handlebars, when he could be out on the water, in the sea air, sailing on one of the most beautiful estuaries in the world."

"I know," said Dave. He felt tongue-tied, he could not explain. He knew it was beautiful, the clubhouse on the creek, the beach of shingle and sand, the red sails on the water. But at the moment it was not what he wanted. He wanted something that he had chosen himself, where he was more on his own, without his dad.

"Have I got to go?" he asked.

"You haven't *got* to," said his father. "But I shall be very disappointed if you don't."

He went for a ride early the next morning, to try to clear his thoughts. He felt mean, he felt he was letting his father down. But he wanted very much to take part in the cycle race, it was the only one that summer. He wished he could do both.

By the time he got back, he had not really decided, though at the back of his mind he knew he would go to the Kermess. His mum was in the kitchen having her breakfast on her own. There was some money on the table and she pushed it towards him. "You'll need this," she said. "For cycling clothes."

"I don't know if I ought to."

"It's what you want to do," she said. "I'd like to see you race. Is it all right if we come along?"

"But what about Dad?"

"I've had a word with him," said his mum. "It won't do him any harm to miss the Commodore's Cup for once."

The entrance to the industrial estate was at one end of the by-pass, and on Sunday it was closed by the police; there was a special constable on duty directing the traffic. Bales of straw had been placed in a semicircle across the road, at the point where the cyclists would be turning, though some of the bales had been moved aside to let riders and competitors' cars through.

Dave arrived on his bike ahead of his parents. He signed in, and a marshal checked his handlebars, saddle and brakes. Then the gear ratio was checked against a measured length on the road, to make sure that it was below the limit for under-sixteen events. He was given a number to pin to his back.

He changed by the roadside into the clothes he had bought the day before at the sports shop in the town. He had chosen a red jersey because it reminded him of the sails of the dinghy, and black cycling shorts. They felt tight and unfamiliar.

He rode around the circuit with the boy from school, to get used to it. After two laps he went along to the entrance to look for his parents. He had been surprised that they wanted to come. He did not mind his mum being there, but he was uneasy about his dad. It made him feel that he had to do well, to prove that it was not just a craze.

When he saw them arrive in the estate car, he directed them away from the public car park, removed a bale of straw, and rode ahead of them down the circuit until they reached the factory car park that the competitors were using.

His dad unpacked. He had brought folding garden chairs, a picnic hamper, some blankets in case it turned cold and a multi-coloured golfing umbrella in case it rained. Laden with all this, they walked along the pavement in front of the wire fence of the factory. David pushed his bicycle along the road and carried the blankets.

They passed a wholesale cash-and-carry. A lot of rubbish, plastic and paper, had blown into the fence and caught in the wire. Mr Robinson poked at it with the golfing umbrella.

"I see now why it's called a Kermess," he said. "Keugh – mess!"

The loudspeaker of the public address system blared out pop music. There was a smell of onions on the air, and they passed a hot-dog van parked in another factory gateway.

Mr Robinson pursed his lips. Dave wanted his dad to like the Kermess, to enjoy and admire it. He suddenly saw it through his eyes, and knew that he hated it.

And yet Dave found the atmosphere intensely exciting. There were bikes everywhere, leaning against the wire fences or lying on the grass verge, in trailers, upright without their front wheels on the roofs of cars. A lot more cyclists were arriving, some in skinsuits in club colours. Some were greasing their legs, rolling up their shorts to avoid the stain of the grease. One was doing leg stretches, and others were warming-up on the track.

They reached the starting line, where quite a few people were already standing or sitting on the grass. There was a family with a tandem and several other bikes against the fence behind them. They all wore cycling gear. The father was quite elderly; he was very tanned, and the muscles stood out on his legs as though he had been cycling all his life.

The Robinsons picked their way through them, and set up their garden chairs. "I wonder what Nigel would say if he could see us here," said Mr Robinson, spreading the blankets over their laps. "He's sailing to the Isle of Wight this afternoon, his boss drove him down to Portsmouth in his Porsche."

He stared at the cyclists on the other side of the road, preparing for their race. "Why do they walk around on tiptoe?" he asked loudly.

"They're wearing cycling shoes," explained Dave. "They fit into the toe-clips."

"They all look deformed to me."

"That's because of their cycling jerseys." They had pockets at the back, stuffed with repair kits and waterproofs.

"I think they look very athletic," said Mrs Robinson.

The music stopped and a commentator began to introduce the afternoon's programme. There were three events, the schoolboys' and schoolgirls' under sixteen, which consisted of six laps of the circuit, a junior event of twelve laps and a senior event, open to anyone over eighteen, of twenty-four laps.

Some of the seniors were already on the track, riding a few laps before their race began. They had started slowly, but gradually built up speed. Three of them had kept together, only a few inches apart, all the way round. They swept by now, and as they passed they created an impression of strength. It was like being close to a powerful machine; it was like standing next to a railway track when an express goes by. Instinctively, Dave glanced at his father to see if he had felt the same thrill.

His dad had a glazed look.

The commentator kept up a constant chatter. He read out a long list of local shops that had sponsored the Kermess by giving prizes. There were bags, caps and shoes, there was a frozen chicken and vouchers for free haircuts, a delicatessen had given a packet of spaghetti.

"Ha!" uttered Mr Robinson.

"And now it's your turn, ladies and gentlemen," the commentator appealed. "The collectors are going around amongst you. These boys and girls are going to slog their guts out for your entertainment this afternoon. Please give generously."

Mr Robinson dug into his pocket, and put a note into the cycling cap held out to him.

The competitors in the under-sixteen race were gathering at the line. The loudspeaker was calling for the track to be cleared, and stewards were going up and down waving all the other cyclists off the circuit.

Dave left his parents and joined the second row, on the outside. He felt that the race would be as much a disappointment to his dad as the rest of the Kermess had been. He would have to watch his son ignominiously losing, when they could have been winning the Commodore's Cup. He knew he had no chance.

Harry, wearing a large yellow badge in his lapel with MARSHAL written across it, gave instructions and warnings. It was a standing start, unlike the time-trials, but the two boys ahead of him already had both feet in their toe-clips, and kept up by balancing against each other.

"Five . . . four . . . three . . . two . . . one – go!" The marshal brought down his flag.

Dave was away with the others, all in a crowd to the straw bales at the turn. But as they came back to the starting line he knew that a bunch of riders had broken away from the rest, amongst them Black-and-Gold, Coconut Oil and one of the two girls in the race. His dad would have something to say about a girl beating him.

There was a rise towards the far end of the circuit, and the tops of his thighs ached as he pedalled up it. Then after the turn there was a glorious swoop down to the level again. The first group had drawn further ahead on the slope, but he was leading the second group. They were using him to set the pace, tiring himself in the lead while they coasted along in his wake. He slowed to let a boy in black and white take the front position, while he followed in the slipstream. Then the two of them took it in turns to lead during the second lap.

He realized how he could salvage something from the race. If he could keep the lead in the second group, he would show his dad that he was serious about cycling.

As they came up to the line at the end of the lap he could hear the voice from the loudspeaker. "Prime, prime, prime," it went.

"Moneymoneymoney . . . A prime of one pound for the first in your group across the line. Prime, prime, prime."

He was following Black-and-White at the time, and tried to pass him. But the other boy held him off and crossed the line a wheel ahead. He could hear the spectators clapping.

There was no prime on the third lap, and the fourth seemed hardest of all. As he forced the pedals around on the rise, with the pain in his thighs getting worse, he wondered why he was doing it. Why choose something so painful? He must want to punish himself, he thought. The feeling of guilt drove him on.

And then he gave up thinking altogether, to become as much like a machine as possible, pumping his legs up and down like pistons.

As he came to the line, the voice of the commentator broke through his daze. "Prime, prime, prime," it called. "A prime for the second group . . . a prime for the rider who can break away."

Again, it was between him and the boy in black and white. He kept close behind his back wheel until the turn. Then as they came out of the bend he stood on his pedals and thrust his bike from side to side. He took the lead, but he had to draw right ahead of the other boy. He kept up the pressure, and glancing behind saw that he had gained a few yards.

By the end of the lap he had increased the distance and was out on his own between the two groups. He pushed on. It seemed easier now that the finish was near. He lapped one of the younger boys and sailed across the line, straightening up and raising both hands off the handlebars.

He freewheeled to a stop. The sweat was pouring down his face, his clothes stuck to him. He felt exhausted but triumphant.

He lay on the grass verge to recover, then joined his parents.

"You did very well," said his mum.

He looked at his dad. He did not care what he said; it would make no difference now, whether he praised or damned.

"Well, we've seen you ride," said his dad. He looked at his watch. "I think we could still get down to the club if we left straightaway."

"You can't," said Dave, who had got his breath back.

"Why not?"

"You can't take the car on to the circuit until all the races are over."

"You're joking."

"It's closed to traffic, you're blocked in."

"But there are two more races to go." The time they would take gradually sank in, and his father looked aghast. "That's thirty-six more laps."

"I'm sorry."

"You did it deliberately."

"I didn't, honestly." Dave laughed. He felt sorry, but not in a guilty sort of way. His dad looked pathetic, his face horror-struck at the thought of having to sit out the rest of a long afternoon at the Kermess.

"Thirty-six more laps," he repeated.

"Never mind," said Dave. "I'll get you a hot dog, on the strength of my winnings."

He could afford to be generous. He had won his prime. He had broken away.

WINGMAN ON ICE

MATT CHRISTOPHER

Matt Christopher is one of America's most popular writers of sports stories for young people. He writes about many major sports, but particularly about ice hockey, the subject of this story. Although Tod plays regularly as a wingman for the White Knights, he lacks confidence in his stick skills. He feels sure that a new stick will bring him better fortune and is delighted when he gets one as a Christmas present. But is it really the answer to his problems?

IT WAS CHRISTMAS MORNING.

Tod and Jane came out of their bedrooms in their pyjamas. Jane ran, screaming happily, for there beside the tree was exactly what she had been wishing for – a sparkling red and white bicycle.

Tod didn't run. He used to run when he was Jane's age. But he was older now. Anyway, his long steps got him there fast enough.

There were big boxes and small boxes piled under the tree, all in fancy wrapping paper and fancy bows. There were also presents that were not wrapped – games, puzzles, and books for him and Jane. These were the gifts Santa Claus had brought. Tod knew the truth about that little fat man in the bright red suit and white whiskers. But Jane didn't. Not everything anyway.

And then he saw the really long gift wrapped beautifully in white and green paper with a wide red ribbon tied around it.

His heart thumped, and he let out a yell as he ran towards it. Just to make sure that the present was his, though, he looked at the small tag tied to it.

For Tod, from Mom and Dad.

It was *it*! He just knew it was!

He tore the beautiful wrapping paper off and there it was. A hockey stick!

He tested its weight. Perfect! He laid the blade against the floor to test its lie. Perfect! He ran his hands up and down its smooth polished surface. Perfect! Everything about it was just *perfect*.

Jane turned from her bicycle and ran towards the door. Mom and Dad were standing just in front of the doorway, wearing their bathrobes and smiling joyfully.

Jane flung her arms around them, and they bent forward and kissed her. Then Tod walked over to them, carrying his hockey stick.

"Thanks, Dad. Thanks, Mom," he said, and gave them both a tight hug. He wasn't able to say anything else. Something in his throat felt ready to burst.

It was a long while later – after they had opened all their presents and given Mom and Dad theirs – when Tod said, "Can I put some tape on it, Dad, and take it to the pond this afternoon?"

"Of course," said Dad. "That's what it's for."

Tod's face was as bright as one of the bulbs on the Christmas tree. "I'll show them when I get on that ice," he said proudly. "You wait and see." He looked up at his dad, eagerness sparkling in his eyes. "You're coming to our game on Saturday morning, aren't you, Dad? We're scrimmaging against the Trojans."

Dad looked at him and shook his head disappointedly. "You know I can't, Tod. I have to be at the department."

"Oh, that's right," said Tod. "Then you won't be able to see any game, will you?"

Dad ruffled his hair. "Maybe I can make an arrangement to get away once or twice," he said. "We'll see."

Dad worked at the Fire Department. His days off were Sundays and Mondays.

"Will you put the tape on it for me, please, Dad?" asked Tod.

"Sure will," said Dad.

They went downstairs into the basement where Dad had a small workshop. Tod took his old, beat-up hockey stick with him for Dad to copy from.

While Dad was wrapping the tape around the blade of the new hockey stick, Tod remembered what Joe Farmer had asked him at the ice pond.

"You used to ski, didn't you, Dad?"

"Yes, I used to ski. Why?"

Tod shrugged. "Well, I remembered Mom saying you did. Was that before you and Mom were married?"

Dad's eyes lifted to Tod's and then returned to his task. "Yes. I skied for a long time, Tod. Started when I was a child, as you with your skating. Got to be fairly good, too. Then I injured my knee and had to give it up."

He shrugged, smiled. He was finished taping the blade of the hockey stick.

"There you are, son. Ready for action."

"Thanks, Dad. Mind if I go to the pond now?"

"Better wait till after dinner," suggested Dad. "That roast beef smells as if it's almost ready to sink our teeth into."

Tod spent almost two hours at the ice pond. Skip, Snowball, Tim, and some other kids were there, too. They admired Tod's new hockey stick. Tod's face beamed with pride. Without a doubt he had the nicest and best hockey stick of them all.

The crowd that assembled at the ice pond did not make it possible for the boys to play scrub, so they passed the puck and dribbled. Tod realized that his passes were better. He dribbled better, too.

At least, he thought so.

Then came Saturday and the scrimmage game with the Trojans at Manna Rink. Mr Farmer, Joe's dad, was at the timekeeper's bench. The game would be played with exactly the same rules as a regular league game. In the Bantam League the teams played two 20-minute periods, not three as in college or professional hockey; high school teams played three 15-minute periods. Line 1 played two 4-minute sessions and

92

Lines 2 and 3 two 3-minute sessions each during each period.

Line 1 of both teams was out on the rink, ready for the referee to drop the puck. The White Knights wore white suits with black trim and the Trojans orange suits with blue and white trim. Their legs looked chubby with shin guards under their long stockings. Sweaters, with stripes on the sleeves and large numbers on the back and small on the front, covered their padded shoulders and elbows. The pants were padded, too. And they all wore padded gloves.

The goalies were especially protected. They wore face masks, chest protectors, huge padded leg guards, and extra-padded goal gloves. The blades of the goal sticks were larger than those used by the other players. Because the sticks received a lot of pounding, they were taped over the heel and partway up the shaft.

Every player wore a helmet. Most of the helmets were of different colours because they were owned by the players. They weren't turned in to the league at the end of the season as the uniforms were.

For a moment there was complete silence. Then the referee dropped the puck in the centre circle of the ice. The game was on.

Joe Farmer, centre, grabbed the puck and passed to his right wingman, Eddie Jones. A Trojan player swept in and intercepted the pass. He dribbled it across the neutral zone, crossed the White Knights' blue line, and headed for the net.

Both defencemen, Al Burns and Duck Franks, went after him. Goalie Jim Smith was crouched, waiting tensely.

Al Burns reached the Trojan first. Al tried to steal the puck and hooked the blade of his stick with the Trojan's. Another Trojan poke-checked the puck and sent it rolling across the ice towards the boards. Duck Franks sped up to it and drove it back up the ice towards Trojans' territory.

Joe Farmer had it for a while, dribbling towards the Trojans' goal. He snapped a shot at it, but the goalie stopped it with his heavy pads for a save and then cleared it away from the net with his stick.

"Be ready, Line 2," said Coach Fillis. He was leaning against the boards in front of the bench where his boys were sitting. In his hand was a clipboard with the roster of the White Knights fastened to it. "Let's see you snap one into that net."

A short time later the buzzer sounded. Line 1 of both teams hurried off the ice, and Line 2 hurried on. Quickly they moved into their positions: Skip Haddock at centre, Tod at right forward, and Jim Wright at left forward. Behind them at right defence was Biff Jones, at left defence Snowball Harry Carr, and goalie Tim Collins.

Pete Sunday, the Trojans' star centre, got the puck away from Skip and passed it to a wingman. Tod moved up quickly, his pumping legs sending chips flying from the blades of this skates. In his hand was the brand new hockey stick, the light twinkling on its shiny surface. This was the moment he had been waiting for. Now he could show what he could do.

Someone bumped into the Trojan wingman and the puck skittered away, free. A mad scramble for it followed. Snowball went down and a Trojan player fell on top of him.

Skip got the puck and started with it across the red line in the centre of the rink. Two Trojans came after him and he passed to Tod. Tod caught it and dribbled it across the Trojans' blue line. He felt so good he could smile. A Trojan defenceman was coming at him, but he didn't care. Tod knew he could out-skate him. And with his new hockey stick he could push that puck wherever he pleased.

He stepped up his speed and gave the puck an extra shove.

Too far! For a second his heart jumped to his throat. He caught up with the puck just before the Trojan player did and tried to glide it lightly ahead of him.

Again too far! He tried to catch up with it, but another Trojan player swept in and took control of it. It was Pete Sunday.

"Thanks, Tod ol' buddy," said Pete, and started to dribble the puck back up the ice, skating close to the boards.

Tod's skates shrieked and shot a stream of ice chips as he came to a stop and bolted back up the ice after Pete. His face was hot as Pete's words rang in his ears.

He came up behind Pete, tried to poke-check the puck.

His skate tangled with Pete's, and down Tod went. He heard Pete laugh as the Trojan centre dribbled the puck towards the White Knights' net.

Quickly, Tod rose to his feet and raced after Pete and the puck. Snowball was already there, trying to take the puck. His stick and Pete's sounded like cracking whips as they smacked against each other.

Then Skip got there – just a fraction of a second before Tod did – and struck Pete with a body check. Pete lost control of the puck, and Skip hooked it with the blade of his stick. Pete charged hard towards Skip, and Tod yelled:

"Here, Skip!"

Skip passed to him. The puck sped like a black bullet. Tod went after it, stuck out his stick.

Missed it! The puck sailed past. Tod, clamping his lips together, whirled and went after it. A Trojan went after it, too. They would meet the puck at the same time.

Tod reached out with his stick. It barely touched the puck.

Tod was so anxious to get the puck that he forgot about the Trojan charging after it, too. They collided solidly. The breath was knocked out of him for an instant, and he fell to the ice. Another orange player came racing towards him.

Tod looked hastily around, saw the puck inches away. He started to swing his stick towards it while still on his knees. Just as he swung, the Trojan tripped over the stick and went flying forwards on his face, skidding almost fifteen feet before he stopped.

A whistle shrilled. Tod paid little attention to it. He got to his feet and dug his skates into the ice, racing after the puck that had been hit towards the boards.

Shreeek! Shreeek! went the whistle again.

"Hold it, Tod!" shouted a voice.

Tod slowed and turned around. The referee was skating swiftly towards the puck.

"Tripping!" he said, touching Tod on the shoulder as he went by. Then he gathered up the puck and skated toward the scorekeeper's bench to inform the scorekeeper of the penalty.

Tod's heart sank. Taking hold of his stick with both hands, he skated slowly off the ice.

"Hurry it up!" snapped the referee.

Tod's neck reddened. He hurried off the ice to the penalty box.

"One minute, Tod," said Mr Farmer.

It seemed a long time before the end of that minute came.

"OK, Tod, get in there, quick," Mr Farmer told him.

Tod got hurriedly back on the ice. But less than thirty seconds later the buzzer sounded, and Line 2 skated off.

After a minute or so Line 3 for the Trojans managed to drive one past the White Knights' goalie for a score. When the White Knights' Line 1 returned to the ice, they tried their best to tie it up, but it was their Line 2 that finally did it. Skip made the goal with Biff getting credit for an assist. Tod did no better during that session than he had the first time.

"You're a little tight out there," said the coach during the intermission. "Keep your hands farther apart. And hit that puck a little easier. Don't look so glum. You'll do all right."

But when Line 2 went in for their turn after intermission, Tod didn't do all right. He missed two passes completely.

There was more scoring this period, with Skip and Snowball sharing two apiece and Biff getting three assists.

The game tied up in the last two minutes. And then the Trojans socked one past Goalie Tim Collins for a beautiful shot that put them ahead. That was the way the game ended, Trojans: 6; White Knights: 5.

All the way home Tod hardly said a word. He was thinking. He had supposed that a brand-new hockey stick would make him play better hockey. He had learned today that this wasn't so. He didn't think he deserved that new hockey stick at all.

Even at home he thought and thought about it. And then he knew what he would do. He would put his new hockey stick away. He wouldn't play with it again until he felt, deep in his heart, that he deserved it.

He stuck it inside the closet of his room. No matter how much he liked it, he wouldn't play with it again until he played a lot better than he did today.

SPIT NOLAN

BILL NAUGHTON

S PIT NOLAN WAS A PAL OF MINE. He was a thin lad with a bony
face that was always pale, except for two rosy spots on his
cheekbones. He had quick brown eyes, short, wiry hair,
rather stooped shoulders, and we all knew that he had only one
lung. He had had a disease which in those days couldn't be
cured, unless you went away to Switzerland, which Spit
certainly couldn't afford. He wasn't sorry for himself in any way,
and in fact we envied him, because he never had to go to school.

Spit was the champion trolley-rider of Cotton Pocket; that was
the district in which we lived. He had a very good balance and
sharp wits, and he was very brave, so that these qualities, when
added to his skill as a rider, meant that no other boy could ever
beat Spit on a trolley – and every lad had one.

Our trolleys were simple vehicles for getting a good ride
downhill at a fast speed. To make one you had to get a stout
piece of wood about five feet in length and eighteen inches wide.
Then you needed four wheels, preferably two pairs, large ones
for the back and smaller ones for the front. However, since we
bought our wheels from the scrapyard, most trolleys had four
odd wheels. Now you had to get a poker and put it in the fire
until it was red hot, and then burn a hole through the wood at

98

the front. Usually it would take three or four attempts to get the hole bored through. Through this hole you fitted the giant nut-and-bolt, which acted as a swivel for the steering. Fastened to the nut was a strip of wood, on to which the front axle was secured by bent nails. A piece of rope tied to each end of the axle served for steering. Then a knob of margarine had to be slanced out of the kitchen to grease the wheels and bearings. Next you had to paint a name on it: *Invincible* or *Dreadnought*, though it might be a motto: *Death before Dishonour* or *Labour and Wait*. That done, you then stuck your chest out, opened the back gate, and wheeled your trolley out to face the critical eyes of the world.

Spit spent most mornings trying out new speed gadgets on his trolley, or searching Enty's scrapyard for good wheels. Afterwards he would go off and have a spin down Cemetery Brew. This was a very steep road that led to the cemetery, and it was very popular with trolley-drivers as it was the only macadamised hill for miles around, all the others being cobblestones for horse traffic. Spit used to lie in wait for a coal-cart or other horse-drawn vehicle, then he would hitch *Egdam* to the back to take it up the brew. *Egdam* was a name in memory of a girl called Madge, whom he had once met at Southport Sanatorium, where he had spent three happy weeks. Only I knew the meaning of it, for he had reversed the letters of her name to keep his love a secret.

It was the custom for lads to gather at the street corner on summer evenings and, trolleys parked at hand, discuss trolleying, road surfaces, and also show off any new gadgets. Then, when Spit gave the sign, we used to set off for Cemetery Brew. There was scarcely any evening traffic on the roads in those days, so that we could have a good practice before our evening race. Spit, the unbeaten champion, would inspect every trolley and rider, and allow a start which was reckoned on the size of the wheels and the weight of the rider. He was always the last in the line of starters, though no matter how long a start he gave it seemed impossible to beat him. He knew that road like the palm of his hand, every tiny lump or pothole, and he never came a cropper.

Among us he took things easy, but when occasion asked for it he would go all out. Once he had to meet a challenge from

Ducker Smith, the champion of the Engine Row gang. On that occasion Spit borrowed a wheel from the baby's pram, removing one nearest the wall, so it wouldn't be missed, and confident he could replace it before his mother took baby out. And after fixing it to his trolley he had made that ride on what was called the "belly-down" style – that is, he lay full stretch on his stomach, so as to avoid wind resistance. Although Ducker got away with a flying start he had not that sensitive touch of Spit, and his frequent bumps and swerves lost him valuable inches, so that he lost the race with a good three lengths. Spit arrived home just in time to catch his mother as she was wheeling young Georgie off the doorstep, and if he had not made a dash for it the child would have fallen out as the pram overturned.

It happened that we were gathered at the street corner with our trolleys one evening when Ernie Haddock let out a hiccup of wonder: "Hey, chaps, wot's Leslie got?"

We all turned our eyes on Leslie Duckett, the plump son of the local publican. He approached us on a brand-new trolley, propelled by flicks of his foot on the pavement. From a distance the thing had looked impressive, but now, when it came up among us, we were too dumbfounded to speak. Such a magnificent trolley had never been seen! The riding board was of solid oak, almost two inches thick; four new wheels with pneumatic tyres; a brake, a bell, a lamp, and a spotless steering-cord. In front was a plate on which was the name in bold lettering: *The British Queen*.

"It's called after the pub," remarked Leslie. He tried to edge it away from Spit's trolley, for it made *Egdam* appear horribly insignificant. Voices had been stilled for a minute, but now they broke out:

"Where'd it come from?"

"How much was it?"

"Who made it?"

Leslie tried to look modest. "My dad had it specially made to measure," he said, "by the gaffer of the Holt Engineering Works."

He was a nice lad, and now he wasn't sure whether to feel proud or ashamed. The fact was, nobody had ever had a trolley made by somebody else. Trolleys were swopped and so on, but no lad had ever owned one that had been made by other hands. We went quiet now, for Spit had calmly turned his attention to it, and was examining *The British Queen* with his expert eye. First he tilted it, so that one of the rear wheels was off the ground, and after giving it a flick of the finger he listened intently with his ear close to the hub.

"A beautiful ball-bearing race," he remarked, "it runs like silk." Next he turned his attention to the body. "Grand piece of timber, Leslie – though a trifle on the heavy side. It'll take plenty of pulling up a brew."

"I can pull it," said Leslie, stiffening.

"You might find it a shade *front-heavy*," went on Spit, "which means it'll be hard on the steering unless you keep it well oiled."

"It's well made," said Leslie. "Eh, Spit?"

Spit nodded. "Aye, all the bolts are counter-sunk," he said, "everything chamfered and fluted off to perfection. But—"

"But what?" asked Leslie.

"Well, it's got none of *you* in it," said Spit.

"How do you mean?" said Leslie.

"Well, you haven't so much as given it a single tap with a hammer," said Spit. "That trolley will be a stranger to you to your dying day."

"How come," said Leslie, "since I *own* it?"

Spit shook his head. "You don't own it," he said, in a quiet, solemn tone. "You own nothing in this world except those things you have taken a hand in the making of, or else you've earned the money to buy them."

Leslie sat down on *The British Queen* to think this one out. We all sat round, scratching our heads.

"You've forgotten to mention one thing," said Ernie Haddock to Spit, "what about the *speed*?"

"Going down a steep hill," said Spit, "she should hold the road well – an' with wheels like that she should certainly be able to shift some."

"Think she could beat *Egdam*?" ventured Ernie.

"That," said Spit, "remains to be seen."

Ernie gave a shout: "A challenge race! *The British Queen* versus *Egdam*!"

"Not tonight," said Leslie. "I haven't got the proper feel of her yet."

"What about Sunday morning?" I said.

Spit nodded. "As good a time as any."

Leslie agreed. "By then," he said in a challenging tone, "I'll be able to handle her."

Chattering like monkeys, eating bread, carrots, fruit, and bits of toffee, the entire gang of us made our way along the silent Sunday-morning streets for the big race at Cemetery Brew. We were split into two fairly equal sides.

Leslie, in his serge Sunday suit, walked ahead, with Ernie Haddock pulling *The British Queen*, and a bunch of supporters around. They were optimistic, for Leslie had easily outpaced every other trolley during the week, though as yet he had not run against Spit.

Spit was in the middle of the group behind, and I was pulling *Egdam* and keeping the pace easy, for I wanted Spit to keep fresh. He walked in and out among us with an air of imperturbability that, considering the occasion, seemed almost godlike. It inspired a fanatical confidence in us. It was such that Chick Dale, a curly headed kid with a soft skin like a girl's, and a nervous lisp, climbed up on to the spiked railings of the cemetery, and, reaching out with his thin fingers, snatched a yellow rose. He ran in front of Spit and thrust it into a small hole in his jersey.

"I pwesent you with the wose of the winner!" he exclaimed.

"And I've a good mind to present you with a clout on the lug," replied Spit, "for pinching a flower from a cemetery. An' what's more, it's bad luck." Seeing Chick's face, he relented. "On second thoughts, Chick, I'll wear it. Ee, wot a 'eavenly smell!"

Happily we went along, and Spit turned to a couple of lads at the back. "Hy, stop that whistling. Don't forget what day it is – folk want their sleep out."

A faint sweated glow had come over Spit's face when we reached the top of the hill, but he was as majestically calm as ever. Taking the bottle of cold water from his trolley seat, he put it to his lips and rinsed out his mouth in the manner of a boxer.

The two contestants were called together by Ernie.

"No bumpin' or borin'," he said.

They nodded.

"The winner," he said, "is the first who puts the nose of his trolley past the cemetery gates."

They nodded.

"Now, who," he asked, "is to be judge?"

Leslie looked at me. "I've no objection to Bill," he said, "I know he's straight."

I hadn't realized I was, I thought, but by heck I will be!

"Ernie here," said Spit, "can be starter."

With that Leslie and Spit shook hands.

"Fly down to them gates," said Ernie to me. He had his father's pigeon-timing watch in his hand. "I'll be setting 'em off dead on the stroke of ten o'clock."

I hurried down to the gates. I looked back and saw the supporters lining themselves on either side of the road. Leslie was sitting upright on *The British Queen*. Spit was settling himself to ride belly-down. Ernie Haddock, handkerchief raised in the right hand, eye gazing down on the watch in the left, was counting them off – just like when he tossed one of his father's pigeons.

"Five – four – three – two – one – *Off!*"

Spit was away like a shot. That vigorous toe push sent him clean ahead of Leslie. A volley of shouts went up from his supporters, and groans from Leslie's. I saw Spit move straight to the middle of the road camber. Then I ran ahead to take up my position at the winning-post.

When I turned again I was surprised to see that Spit had not increased the lead. In fact, it seemed that Leslie had begun to gain on him. He had settled himself into a crouched position, and those perfect wheels combined with his extra weight were bringing him up with Spit. Not that it seemed possible he could ever catch him. For Spit, lying flat on his trolley, moving with a fine balance, gliding, as it were, over the rough patches, looked to me as though he were a bird that might suddenly open out its wings and fly clean into the air.

The runners along the side could no longer keep up with the trolleys. And now, as they skimmed past the halfway mark, and came to the very steepest part, there was no doubt that Leslie was gaining. Spit had never ridden better; he coaxed *Egdam* over the tricky parts, swayed with her, gave her her head, and guided her. Yet Leslie, clinging grimly to the steering-rope of *The British Queen*, and riding the rougher part of the road, was actually drawing level. Those beautiful ball-bearing wheels, engineer-made, encased in oil, were holding the road, and bringing Leslie along faster than spirit and skill could carry Spit.

Dead level they sped into the final stretch. Spit's slight figure was poised fearlessly on his trolley, drawing the extremes of speed from her. Thundering beside him, anxious but determined, came Leslie. He was actually drawing ahead – and forcing his way to the top of the camber. On they came like two charioteers – Spit delicately edging to the side, to gain inches by the extra downward momentum. I kept my eyes fastened clean across the road as they came belting past the winning-post.

First past was the plate *The British Queen*. I saw that first. Then I saw the heavy rear wheel jog over a pothole and strike Spit's front wheel – sending him in a swerve across the road. Suddenly then, from nowhere, a charabanc came speeding round the wide bend.

Spit was straight in its path. Nothing could avoid the collision. I gave a cry of fear as I saw the heavy solid tyre of the front wheel hit the trolley. Spit was flung up and his back hit the radiator. Then the driver stopped dead.

I got there first. Spit was lying on the macadam road on his side. His face was white and dusty, and coming out between his lips and trickling down his chin was a rivulet of fresh red blood. Scattered all about him were yellow rose petals.

"Not my fault," I heard the driver shouting. "I didn't have a chance. He came straight at me."

The next thing we were surrounded by women who had got out of the charabanc. And then Leslie and all the lads came up.

"Somebody send for an ambulance!" called a woman.

"I'll run an' tell the gatekeeper to telephone," said Ernie Haddock.

"I hadn't a chance," the driver explained to the women.

"A piece of his jersey on the starting-handle there . . ." said someone.

"Don't move him," said the driver to a stout woman who had bent over Spit. "Wait for the ambulance."

"Hush up," she said. She knelt and put a silk scarf under Spit's head. Then she wiped his mouth with her little handkerchief.

He opened his eyes. Glazed they were, as though he couldn't see. A short cough came out of him, then he looked at me and his lips moved.

"Who won?"

"Thee!" blurted out Leslie. "Tha just licked me. Eh, Bill?"

"Aye," I said, "old *Egdam* just pipped *The British Queen*."

Spit's eyes closed again. The women looked at each other. They nearly all had tears in their eyes. Then Spit looked up again, and his wise, knowing look came over his face. After a minute he spoke in a sharp whisper:

"Liars. I can remember seeing Leslie's back wheel hit my front 'un. I didn't win – I lost." He stared upward for a few seconds, then his eyes twitched and shut.

The driver kept repeating how it wasn't his fault, and next thing the ambulance came. Nearly all the women were crying now, and I saw the look that went between the two men who put Spit on a stretcher – but I couldn't believe he was dead. I had to go into the ambulance with the attendant to give him particulars. I went up the step and sat down inside and looked out the little window as the driver slammed the doors. I saw the driver holding Leslie as a witness. Chick Dale was lifting the smashed-up *Egdam* on to the body of *The British Queen*. People with bunches of flowers in their hands stared after us as we drove off. Then I heard the ambulance man asking me Spit's name. Then he touched me on the elbow with his pencil and said:

"Where *did* he live?"

I knew then. That word "did" struck right into me. But for a minute I couldn't answer. I had to think hard, for the way he said it made it suddenly seem as though Spit Nolan had been dead and gone for ages.

THE BLUE DARTER

JUDITH LOGAN LEHNE

I STOOD IN A CORNER OF THE DUGOUT, making circles in the dirt with my shoe, just listening.

"We *gave* them the game," Lyle said. His hair and his "Team Captain" shirt were soaked with sweat. "We played terrible."

Paul nodded and pointed his finger at Julio. "You call yourself a pitcher? You practically threw the ball right at their bats!"

"Everybody has a bad day," I said to Lyle. "Why didn't you put Lindsay in? Her Blue Darter pitch was just what we needed today." Lindsay looked over at me, and her eyes seemed to say thanks.

"Get real, Jonathan," Lyle said, moving a huge wad of gum inside his cheek. "It's bad enough I let you talk us into having a girl on the team. The Orioles would've laughed us off the field if we had let her pitch."

Lindsay pulled off her cap and shook out her long ponytail. "The score was 18 to 6, Lyle!" she said. "The Orioles got their laughs anyway."

"Well, the Cubs won't be laughing tomorrow," Lyle said. He grabbed his mitt. "Let's practise!"

Everyone tromped to the field.

"Jonathan," Paul said, "you're our best hitter. Tell us your secret."

107

"Natural talent," I said, shrugging. I felt Lindsay's eyes on me. I knew what she wanted me to tell them. I owed my batting success to her – and the hours of practice with her grandfather. He's the one who taught her the Blue Darter. I never got the hang of it, but Lindsay could whistle the ball off her fingers and make it curve crazily when I was in mid-swing. It was because of Lindsay's Blue Darter that I was a good batter. But I couldn't tell the guys that. I just couldn't.

Walking home, Lindsay was silent. When we reached her house, she turned and glared.

"You could have told them, Jonathan," she said between clenched teeth. "Maybe they'd have let me pitch tomorrow."

I glared back. "You want me to make a fool of myself? When you're not around, they always tease me. If they knew you helped my batting . . ."

She looked as though she might cry, but I kept yelling. "I got you on the team. Isn't that enough?"

"This isn't about *baseball*," she said. Her ponytail whipped across her face as she stomped away.

All night I kept hearing Lindsay saying, "This isn't about baseball." What did she mean?

Before the game with the Cubs, I apologized to her. "It's OK," she said. "I guess it's not easy having a girl for a best friend."

Listening to Lyle, the guys squirmed on the bench. Lindsay leaned against the dugout wall.

"Show 'em our best! No errors," Lyle said, blowing bubbles between words. "Julio, you pitch."

I looked at Lindsay, but I kept quiet.

We were first at bat. The Cubs' pitcher was good, but not great. When I stepped to the plate, Lyle was on third and Paul was on first. I looked at the dugout. Lindsay shouted, "Whack it!" My hands felt clammy.

"Strike one!" the umpire shouted. I hadn't even swung at it.

"Concentrate," I said to myself. The ball came towards the plate, and I swung. *Crack!* I raced to first . . . second . . . third . . . home!

After the back-slapping cheers, the game took a downward turn. The Cubs' not-so-great pitcher got better, and our hitting

108

got worse. Julio was still in a pitching slump. By the fifth inning, we were down by seven runs.

As we took the field. I grabbed Lyle's arm. "Give Lindsay a chance," I said. The team stopped to listen. Lindsay stayed in the dugout, watching.

"No girl pitchers," Lyle snarled. "Especially not your *girlfriend*."

"She's not my—" I began. I looked at Lindsay. This isn't about baseball, she'd said.

"She is my girl *friend*," I said. Someone snickered. "She's a girl, and she's my friend." I put my face close to Lyle's. "And when you see her Blue Darter pitch, you will know she's this *team's* friend, too."

"Let her pitch," Julio said.

Talking all at once, the guys nudged Lyle. "Let's see her Blue Darter!"

Lyle called Lindsay from the dugout. "You'd better be good," he said.

Lindsay stepped to the mound. "Come on, Lindsay," I cheered. "Show 'em your stuff."

She kicked dirt around, looking shy and not at all like a pitcher. The guys exchanged glances. Just wait, I wanted to tell them. They didn't have to wait long. She bent forward, threw her arm back, and whipped the ball off her fingers. It flew like an arrow until it was nearly over the plate, then it veered to the left.

"Strike one!" the umpire called.

Lindsay grinned at me and continued to hurl the Blue Darter at lightning speed, just as her grandfather had taught her. The Cubs never even scored another run.

We lost, but the Cubs weren't laughing.

Lyle came into the dugout and shook Lindsay's hand. He swallowed hard. "You're a terrific pitcher," he said. He turned to me. "And you've got a great best friend."

"I know," I said, looking at Lindsay. "True blue."

TOM BROWN'S SCHOOL DAYS

THOMAS HUGHES

Tom Brown's School Days *was written in 1857. Its setting is the public school Rugby (under the headmastership of the esteemed Dr Arnold), where the game began. This extract describes how rugby was originally played. There were two sets of goalposts with a crossbar, between and over which the ball had to be kicked for a team to score a point. The game had an unlimited number of players and often lasted for hours. The match depicted here features the School-house (which includes new boy Tom Brown) – against the whole of the rest of the school! The game is described as if it were a war – and certainly it's very physical.*

"HOLD THE PUNT-ABOUT!" "To the goals!" are the cries, and all stray balls are impounded by the authorities; and the whole mass of boys move up towards the two goals, dividing as they go into three bodies. That little band on the left, consisting of from fifteen to twenty boys, Tom amongst them, who are making for the goal under the School-house wall, are the School-house boys who are not to play-up, and have to stay in goal. The larger body moving to the island goal, are the schoolboys in a like predicament. The great mass in the middle are the players-up, both sides mingled together; they are hanging their jackets, and all who mean real work, their hats, waistcoats, neck-handkerchiefs, and braces, on the railings round the small trees; and there they go by twos and threes up to their respective grounds. There is none of the colour and tastiness of get-up, you will perceive, which lends such a life to the present game at Rugby, making the dullest and worst-fought match a pretty sight. Now each house has its own uniform of cap and jersey, of some lively colour: but at the time we are speaking of, plush caps have not yet come in, or uniforms of any sort, except the School-house white trousers, which are abominably cold today: let us get to work, bare-headed and girded with our plain leather straps – but we mean business, gentlemen.

And now that the two sides have fairly sundered, and each occupies its own ground, and we get a good look at them, what absurdity is this? You don't mean to say that those fifty or sixty boys in white trousers, many of them quite small, are going to play that huge mass opposite? Indeed, I do, gentlemen; they're going to try at any rate, and won't make such a bad fight of it either, mark my word; for hasn't old Brooke won the toss with his lucky halfpenny, and got choice of goals and kick-off? The new ball you may see lie there quite by itself, in the middle, pointing towards the School or island goal; in another minute it will be well on its way there. Use that minute in remarking how the School-house side is drilled. You will see in the first place that the sixth-form boy, who has the charge of goal, has spread his force (the goalkeepers) so as to occupy the whole space behind the goalposts, at distances of about five yards apart; a safe and well-kept goal is the foundation of all good play. Old Brooke is talking to the captain of quarters; and now he moves away; see how that youngster spreads his men (the light brigade) carefully over the ground, halfway between their own goal and the body of their own players-up (the heavy brigade). These again play in several bodies; there is young Brooke and the bull-dogs – mark them well – they are the "fighting brigade", the "die-hards", larking about at leap-frog to keep themselves warm, and playing tricks on one another. And on each side of old Brooke, who is now standing in the middle of the ground and just going to kick-off, you see a separate wing of players-up, each with a boy of acknowledged prowess to look to – here Warner, and there, Hedge; but over all is old Brooke, absolute as he of Russia, but wisely and bravely ruling over willing and worshipping subjects, a true football king. His face is earnest and careful as he glances a last time over his array, but full of pluck and hope, the sort of look I hope to see in my general when I go out to fight.

The School side is not organized in the same way. The goalkeepers are all in lumps, any-how and no-how; you can't distinguish between the players-up and the boys in quarters, and there is divided leadership; but with such odds in strength and weight it must take more than that to hinder them from winning; and so their leaders seem to think, for they let the players-up manage themselves.

But now look, there is a slight move forward of the School-house wings; a shout of "Are you ready?" and loud, affirmative reply. Old Brooke takes half a dozen quick steps, and away goes the ball spinning towards the School goal; seventy yards before it touches ground, and at no point above twelve or fifteen feet high, a model kick-off; and the School-house cheer and rush on; the ball is returned, and they meet it, and drive it back amongst the masses of the School already in motion. Then the two sides close, and you can see nothing for minutes but a swaying crowd of boys, at one point violently agitated. That is where the ball is, and there are the keen players to be met, and the glory and the hard knocks to be got: you hear the dull thud, thud of the ball, and the shouts of "Off your side," "Down with him," "Put him over," "Bravo." This is what we call a scrummage, gentlemen, and the first scrummage in a School-house match was no joke in the consulship of Plancus.

But see! It has broken; the ball is driven out on the School-house side, and a rush of the School carries it past the School-house players-up. "Look out in quarters," Brooke's and twenty other voices ring out; no need to call tho', the School-house captain of quarters has caught it on the bound, dodges the foremost School boys, who are heading the rush, and sends it back with a good drop-kick well into the enemy's country. And then follows rush upon rush, and scrummage upon scrummage, the ball now driven through into the School-house quarters, and

113

now into the School goal; for the School-house have not lost the advantage which the kick-off and a slight wind gave them at the outset, and are slightly "penning" their adversaries. You say, you don't see much in it all; nothing but a struggling mass of boys, and a leather ball, which seems to excite them all to great fury, as a red rag does a bull. My dear sir, a battle would look much the same to you, except that the boys would be men, and the balls iron; but a battle would be worth your looking at for all that, and so is a football match. You can't be expected to appreciate the delicate strokes of play, the turns by which a game is lost and won – it takes an old player to do that, but the broad philosophy of football you can understand if you will. Come along with me a little nearer, and let us consider it together.

The ball has just fallen again where the two sides are thickest, and they close rapidly around it in a scrummage; it must be driven through now by force or skill, till it flies out on one side or the other. Look how differently the boys face it! Here come two of the bull-dogs, bursting through the outsiders; in they go, straight to the heart of the scrummage, bent on driving that ball out on the opposite side. That is what they mean to do. My sons, my sons! You are too hot; you have gone past the ball, and must struggle now right through the scrummage, and get round and back again to your own side before you can be of any further use. Here comes young Brooke; he goes in as straight as you, but keeps his head and backs and bends, holding himself still behind the ball, and driving it furiously when he gets the chance. Take a leaf out of his book, you young chargers. Here come Speedicut and Flashman, the School-house bully, with shouts and great action. Won't you two come up to young Brooke, after locking-up, by the School-house fire, with "Old fellow, wasn't that just a splendid scrummage by the three trees!" But he knows you, and so do we. You don't really want to drive that ball through that scrummage, chancing all hurt for the glory of the School-house – but to make us think that's what you want – a vastly different thing; and fellows of your kidney will never go through more than the skirts of a scrummage, where it's all push and no kicking. We respect boys who keep out of it, and don't sham going in; but you – we had rather not say what we think of you.

Then the boys who are bending and watching on the outside, mark them – they are most useful players, the dodgers; who seize the ball the moment it rolls out from amongst the chargers, and away with it across to the opposite goal; they seldom go into the scrummage, but must have more coolness than the chargers: as endless as are boys' characters, so are their ways of facing or not facing a scrummage at football.

Three-quarters of an hour are gone; first winds are failing, and weight and numbers beginning to tell. Yard by yard the School-house have been driven back, contesting every inch of ground. The bull-dogs are the colour of mother earth from shoulder to ankle, except young Brooke, who has a marvellous knack of keeping his legs. The School-house are being penned in their turn, and now the ball is behind their goal, under the Doctor's wall. The Doctor and some of his family are there looking on, and seem as anxious as any boy for the success of the School-house. We get a minute's breathing time before old Brooke kicks out, and he gives the word to play strongly for touch, by the three trees. Away goes the ball, and the bull-dogs after it, and in another minute there is shout of "In touch," "Our ball." Now's your time, old Brooke, while your men are still fresh. He stands with the ball in his hand, while the two sides form in deep lines opposite one another: he must strike it straight out between them. The lines are thickest close to him, but young Brooke and two or three of his men are shifting up further, where the opposite line is weak. Old Brooke strikes it out straight and strong, and it falls opposite his brother. Hurra! That rush has taken it right through the School line, and away past the three trees, far into their quarters, and young Brooke and the bull-dogs are close upon it. The School leaders rush back shouting "Look out in goal," and strain every nerve to catch him, but they are after the fleetest foot in Rugby. There they go straight for the School goalposts, quarters scattering before them. One after another the bull-dogs go down, but young Brooke holds on. "He is down." No! A long stagger, but the danger is past; that was the shock of Crew, the most dangerous of dodgers. And now he is close to the School goal, the ball not three yards before him. There is a hurried rush of the School fags to the spot, but no one throws himself on the ball, the only chance, and young Brooke has touched it right under the School goalposts.

The School leaders come up furious, and administer toco to the wretched fags nearest at hand; they may well be angry, for it is all Lombard-street to a china orange that the School-house kick a goal with the ball touched in such a good place. Old Brooke of course will kick it out, but who shall catch and place it? Call Crab Jones. Here he comes, sauntering along with a straw in his mouth, the queerest, coolest fish in Rugby: if he were tumbled into the moon this minute, he would just pick himself up without taking his hands out of his pockets or turning a hair. But it is a moment when the boldest charger's heart beats quick. Old Brooke stands with the ball under his arm motioning the School back; he will not kick out till they are all in goal, behind the posts; they are all edging forwards, inch by inch, to get nearer for the rush at Crab Jones, who stands there in front of old Brooke to catch the ball. If they can reach and destroy him before he catches, the danger is over; and with one and the same rush they will carry it right away to the School-house goal. Fond hope! It is kicked out and caught beautifully. Crab strikes his heel into the ground, to mark the spot where the ball was caught, beyond which the School line may not advance; but there they stand, five deep, ready to rush the moment the ball touches the ground. Take plenty of room! Don't give the rush a chance of reaching you! Place it true and steady! Trust Crab Jones – he has made a small hole with his heel for the ball to lie on, by which he is resting on one knee, with his eye on old Brooke. "Now!" Crab places the ball at the word, old Brooke kicks, and it rises slowly and truly as the School rush forward.

Then a moment's pause, while both sides look up at the spinning ball. There it flies, straight between the two posts, some five feet above the crossbar, an unquestioned goal; and a shout of real genuine joy rings out from the School-house players-up, and a faint echo of it comes over the close from the goalkeepers

under the Doctor's wall. A goal in the first hour – such a thing hasn't been done in the School-house match this five years.

"Over!" is the cry: the two sides change goals, and the School-house goalkeepers come threading their way across through the masses of the School; the most openly triumphant of them, amongst whom is Tom, a School-house boy of two hours' standing, getting their ears boxed in the transit. Tom indeed is excited beyond measure, and it is all the sixth-form boy, kindest and safest of goalkeepers, has been able to do to keep him from rushing out whenever the ball has been near their goal. So he holds him by his side, and instructs him in the science of touching.

At this moment, Griffith, the itinerant vendor of oranges from Hill Morton, enters the close with his heavy baskets; there is a rush of small boys upon the little pale-faced man, the two sides mingling together, subdued by the great Goddess Thirst, like the English and French by the streams in the Pyrenees. The leaders are past oranges and apples, but some of them visit their coats, and apply innocent looking ginger-beer bottles to their mouths. It is no ginger-beer though, I fear, and will do you no good. One short mad rush, and then a stitch in the side, and no more honest play; that's what comes of those bottles.

But now Griffith's baskets are empty, the ball is placed again midway, and the School are going to kick off. Their leaders have sent their lumber into goal, and rated the rest soundly, and one hundred and twenty picked players-up are there, bent on retrieving the game. They are to keep the ball in front of the School-house goal, and then to drive it in by sheer strength and weight. They mean heavy play and no mistake, and so old Brooke sees; and places Crab Jones in quarters just before the goal, with four or five picked players, who are to keep the ball away to the sides, where a try at goal, if obtained, will be less dangerous than in front. He himself, and Warner and Hedge, who have saved themselves till now, will lead the charges.

"Are you ready?" "Yes." And away comes the ball kicked high in the air, to give the School time to rush on and catch it as it falls. And here they are amongst us. Meet them like Englishmen, you

School-house boys, and charge them home. Now is the time to show what mettle is in you – and there shall be a warm seat by the hall fire, and honour, and lots of bottled beer tonight, for him who does his duty in the next half-hour. And they are well met. Again and again the cloud of their players-up gathers before our goal, and comes threatening on, and Warner or Hedge, with young Brooke and the relics of the bull-dogs, break through and carry the ball back; and old Brooke ranges the field like Job's war-horse; the thickest scrummage parts asunder before his rush, like the waves before a clipper's bows; his cheery voice rings over the field, and his eye is everywhere. And if these miss the ball, and it rolls dangerously in front of our goal, Crab Jones and his men have seized it and sent it away towards the sides with the unerring drop-kick. This is worth living for; the whole sum of schoolboy existence gathered up into one straining, struggling half-hour, a half-hour worth a year of common life.

The quarter to five has struck, and the play slackens for a minute before goal; but here is Crew, the artful dodger, driving the ball in behind our goal, on the island side, where our quarters are weakest. Is there no one to meet him? Yes! Look at little East! The ball is just at equal distances between the two, and they rush together, the young man of seventeen and the boy of twelve, and kick it at the same moment. Crew passes on without a stagger; East is hurled forward by the shock, and plunges on his shoulder, as if he would bury himself in the ground; but the ball rises straight into the air, and falls behind Crew's back, while the "bravos" of the School-house attest the pluckiest charge of all that hard-fought day. Warner picks East up lame and half stunned, and he hobbles back into goal, conscious of having played the man.

And now the last minutes are come, and the School gather for their last rush every boy of the hundred and twenty who has a run left in him. Reckless of the defence of their own goal, on they come across the level big-side ground, the ball well down amongst them, straight for our goal, like the column of the Old Guard up the slope at Waterloo. All former charges have been child's play to this. Warner and Hedge have met them, but still on they come. The bull-dogs rush in for the last time; they are hurled over or carried back, striving hand, foot, and eyelids. Old Brooke comes sweeping round the skirts of the play, and turning short round, picks out the very heart of the scrummage, and plunges in. It wavers for a moment – he has the ball! No, it has passed him, and his voice rings out clear over the advancing tide, "Look out in goal." Crab Jones catches it for a moment; but before he can kick, the rush is upon him and passes over him; and he picks himself up behind them with his straw in his mouth, a little dirtier, but as cool as ever.

The ball rolls slowly in behind the School-house goal not three yards in front of a dozen of the biggest School players-up.

There stand the School-house præpostor, safest of goalkeepers, and Tom Brown by his side, who has learned his trade by this time. Now is your time, Tom. The blood of all the Browns is up, and the two rush in together, and throw themselves on the ball, under the very feet of the advancing column; the præpostor on his hands and knees arching his back, and Tom all along on his face. Over them topple the leaders of the rush, shooting over the back of the præpostor but falling flat on Tom, and knocking all the wind out of his small carcase. "Our ball," says the præpostor, rising with his prize; "but get up there, there's a little fellow under you." They are hauled and rolled off him, and Tom is discovered a motionless body.

Old Brooke picks him up. "Stand back, give him air," he says; and then feeling his limbs, adds, "No bones broken. How do you feel, young 'un?"

"Hah-hah," gasps Tom as his wind comes back, "pretty well, thank you – all right."

"Who is he?" says Brooke.

"Oh, it's Brown; he's a new boy; I know him," says East coming up.

"Well, he is a plucky youngster, and will make a player," says Brooke.

And five o'clock strikes. "No side" is called, and the first day of the School-house match is over.

BASKETBALL GAME

*One of the most refreshing aspects of sport is its power to break down barriers.
In this story, the barrier is one of race. Allen, a black teenager, moves with his
family to a town in the southern states of America where racial tension is high
– and prejudice can lead to life-threatening violence. Despite the danger, Allen
plays basketball with the white girl next door . . .*

EVERY SATURDAY Allen's parents went shopping. Allen usually went too, but this Saturday he decided to stay home. They hadn't been gone long when he went out to the driveway, the basketball under his arm. As he played he was very conscious of every basket he made. He practised shooting with his left hand and made more than he missed. He wanted to be good with either hand. Although he never looked towards her house, he presumed she was watching. At least she knew he was there. The sound of the ball hitting the backboard and bouncing on the driveway couldn't be ignored, and it wasn't long before he heard a door slam.

He looked around and saw her running across the backyard.

"Hi, Allen!"

"Hi!" he returned, smiling shyly. He looked at her teeth and was surprised to see the metal gone. And for the first time he thought she was pretty. Not as pretty as Ingrid or Gloria, but pretty nonetheless. Her brown hair was cut short and hung down around her ears. Her face was round and she had thin lips. But what fascinated him most were her eyes. He'd noticed them before and sometimes he thought they were brown, but other times they appeared to be green. This morning they looked yellow. He wished that he had eyes that changed colours. His eyes were so dark that one didn't know if they were brown or black. He wasn't sure himself.

"Can I play some ball with you?"

"Sure."

She climbed over the low fence. "You're going to beat me, I know. You're so good."

"I'm not good. And it's easy when there's nobody playing but you." He sounded more at ease with her than he really was. He wanted to turn around to see if anyone was looking but stopped himself. If you pretended everything was normal, well, maybe it would be. He threw the ball to her and she bounced it clumsily a couple of times and shot it towards the basket. It hit the rim and bounced away. Allen chased it up the driveway and threw it back to her. "Take another one." She bounced the ball and shot again, awkwardly thrusting her arms out and releasing the ball. It bounced off the rim and on to the lawn, hitting the clothesline pole. Allen picked the ball up, dribbled back on the driveway, spun around, jumped, and shot. The ball bounced off the backboard, hit the front of the rim, and ricocheted off.

"Seems like I brought you bad luck."

"Oh, I miss more often than you think," he conceded.

They took turns shooting for a while and eventually Rebecca made a basket. "You want to play a game?" she asked.

He looked surprised. "Sure."

"I know you're going to beat me."

"Don't be too sure," he said, knowing he was going to beat her. "You take it out of bounds first." He pointed up the driveway to a drainpipe hanging down the side of the house. "That's out. The fence is out and the grass is out. OK?"

"OK."

Rebecca bounced the ball clumsily down the driveway. Several times she double dribbled but Allen didn't say anything. It didn't make any difference since he knew he could beat her. She slowly made her way towards the basket, Allen waving his hands in front of her face. He could have easily stolen the ball from her but didn't. She stopped dribbling, grabbed the ball, and drove towards the basket. Instead of jumping with her to block the shot, Allen moved back and she scored.

"You just let me do that," she told him.

He didn't say anything, not sure why he'd let her do it. He took the ball up the driveway and began dribbling back towards the basket. Rebecca guarded him closely, slapping at the ball several times and missing, but hitting his arm. He maintained control of the ball, and as he leapt to shoot she pushed him, knocking him down. His shot didn't go in.

"Hey, that's a foul," he said, getting up slowly.

"Oh, we ain't playing by the rules, are we? You know you're lots better than I am. I have to do something to try and even things up, don't I? And anyway, you're a boy."

That was true, he thought, so he brushed himself off as Rebecca took the ball out of bounds. But each time she went in for a lay-up, which was the only shot she knew, Allen found himself moving aside and letting her make it. And everytime he had the ball, she pushed him, bumped him, and did anything she could to distract him. He wanted to do the same to her, but for some reason he couldn't.

"I won!" she shouted happily. "I beat you! Let's play another game."

He shook his head. "Uh-uh, I don't want to get beat twice in one day."

"Chicken!" she teased, pushing him playfully. Just then they heard what they thought was a car pulling into her driveway. It was on the other side of her house and they couldn't see it. "Gotta go, Allen. Maybe I'll see you later." And before he could reply, she was leaping over the low fence and running across her yard. Just before she went into her house she waved to him. He waved back and had just lowered his hand when he saw her father's car come into view and stop in front of their garage. Allen pretended to be examining his basketball as Rebecca's parents got out of their car.

He wondered if her father had said something to her about him. The way she'd jumped over the fence and run in the house when they heard the car made him think that her father didn't want her talking to him any more than his father wanted him talking to her. Yet she'd come over that morning anyway. She acted like she didn't care what her father thought. And as long as she acted that way, Allen knew he couldn't act any differently. She wasn't afraid of him, so why should he be afraid of her?

TALK US THROUGH IT

MICHAEL HARDCASTLE

"Listen," was the way James Boston always began his stories; and usually people did because he talked so well.

"Listen," he'd say, "what d'you think of this? Great, eh?" Then, after a pause to make sure everyone was paying attention and to gather his breath, he'd launch into his latest commentary, his eyes closing occasionally as if to see all the action in close-up.

"Listen," he said now, "Heeson jinks past the United left-back, looks up, hesitates a moment – very cool indeed – and the cross comes over. A United player fails to intercept, and Cornish is there and Cornish pulls the ball down – shoots! – and Cornish has SCORED! Oh, great goal – beautifully executed – right into the top corner of the net. And Cornish wheels away as the crowd goes mad. But, wait a second. Oh no! The referee's signalling it wasn't a goal after all. He's disallowed it. Well, that's a sensation. Heeson simply cannot believe it. He's protesting, well, pretty vigorously you'd have to say – yes, protesting vigorously to the referee. But the ref doesn't want to know. I can tell you, it's no goal. So the score remains—"

James paused, eyes still agleam with the excitement of his commentary. "Go on, then," he urged. "What did you think of that?"

"Well, not bad, but not one of your greatest," said Peter Colne candidly. Peter was one of James's fans but he didn't like to admit it, let alone show it. Best of all was when he himself was included in a commentary as James described him bringing off one of his crunching tackles or thunderous clearances. He cherished the line where "Colne charged in like an unstoppable bulldozer". Unhappily, James hadn't repeated that for a long time.

"Jimbo, do us the one where the ref fell over the ball and got kicked in the head," Xavier pleaded. "Just like it happened to that ref at the City–Everton game."

James glared at him. He hated anyone tinkering with his name. Xavier was so pleased with his own name he felt he could be careless with anyone else's whenever he wished. "I don't do funny ones now," he stated.

Xavier's eyebrows shot up. "Since when, Jimbo?"

"Since I decided to become a professional broadcaster, that's when," was the somewhat startling reply. Then he added: "There's a competition next month to find new talent for the BBC commentary team in this region. And I'm going to win it. So I'm only interested in the serious stuff from now on, OK?"

"You've no chance," Xavier declared. "They wouldn't want anyone of our age, that's obvious."

"No, it's not," James insisted. "They're covering junior matches now, schoolboy internationals, that sort of thing. So they want a young person's view, a young voice. Most of the present commentators are geriatrics. And I'm the best young presenter by miles. I mean, I *really* know the game."

Nobody, not even Xavier, disputed that. It was recognized that James knew the laws of football as well as almost any referee. Whenever there was so much as a hint of a disagreement affecting their play he was the one consulted: and his ruling was accepted without demur.

That evening he'd just switched on the first of his favourite videos when his mother looked in. "Not football tonight as well!" she protested. "You must have *some* homework to do."

"This is it," James said, interrupting his commentary. "I'm swatting up like mad."

"Listen," she said loudly, "I'm telling you for your own good: there's more to life than football. You've got to get down to work and prepare yourself for a real job."

"Football's going to be my real job. When the World Cup comes round the year after next that's where I'll be, sitting behind a microphone, talking to *the world*. That's what I'm doing now, rehearsing."

She left with one of her exaggerated sighs. It was a pity James's father was not around to talk some sense into him.

After switching off his bed light James concentrated on his favourite footage before falling asleep, letting the silent scenes flicker through his mind while he provided the vivid words. He'd told no one that the competition was being held the following evening, so if disaster struck he wouldn't have to furnish wholesale excuses. Unusually, he would be speechless.

At school next day he was twice admonished for being inattentive in a drama lesson. Miss Sales, concerned, asked if he felt unwell. "It's not like you to be so, so *uninterested*. You also look, well, quite pale."

"I'm fine, miss, really," he tried to assure his favourite teacher who, he knew, also favoured him. "Just a bit, well, wound-up, somehow."

Fortunately, she didn't pry. "Aren't we all?" was all she said.

He didn't go home for tea because he didn't want to attempt a commentary on a full stomach (a tip he'd heard from a professional). He'd warned his mother he was going to a friend's so he wouldn't be missed. Before going to the studio he wandered round the TV and music department of a store in the hope of finding a football match on one of the banks of screens on display. He was out of luck and so his final rehearsal on the street was total fiction.

He'd often stood on the corner opposite the building which housed the studio on the first floor and it didn't impress him any more now than it had in the past. At street level were the most outdated men's outfitters in the world, a stained glass workshop, a frozen food "emporium", as it described itself, and a hairdressing salon (female not even unisex).

The entrance to the cold stone steps leading to the upper floor was narrow and littered with crushed cans, thrown-away take-away boxes and some unmentionable items of flotsam. In James's opinion, a BBC studio should be fronted by plate-glass and a servile, uniformed doorman. At the top of the stairs a frizzy-haired girl peered short-sightedly at him from behind a glass-partitioned counter. He straightened the football supporters' tie he believed would impress the judging panel and gave his name.

"Oh, they won't want you for twenty minutes yet, at least," she told him. "They're on the line to London – in conference, you know. Just sit over there. You can read any of those mags you like."

One glance told him they were as boring as the waiting-room. Really, he wanted someone to talk to but Frizzy-hair was doubly employed, talking on the telephone clamped between shoulder and ear while riffling through a pile of files. James hated to have to wait to begin anything. Already he could feel that his mouth was beginning to dry up as, mentally, he revised some of his best phrases. If these people chose a starting time why didn't they stick to it? Oh, and where were the other candidates in the competition? Was one of them being tested now and proving so good they were giving him extra time? Even being *congratulated* by the judge? James bit his lip. No, no, don't be crazy, he told himself. That's not the way the BBC would do things.

Then, almost unexpectedly, a tall, thin man with a sharply pointed beard opened a door into the waiting-room and inquired pleasantly: "Mr Boston, is it? I'm sorry we've kept you waiting. Would you be good enough to come this way? I'm Roger Richardson, by the way."

Bemused by the suddenness with which things were happening, James shook the proffered hand and followed the man into what he recognised from his researches as a real studio with the entire wall to the left taken up by a window looking into a control room. He was asked to take a seat at a round table in the centre of which was an upright microphone. His companion, however, produced what he called a "throat mike" and asked James whether he'd ever worn one before.

"Er, no, not really, well, I mean, I don't, er, think so." He knew he sounded ridiculous and he must be giving the worst possible impression of a nervous, mindless *idiot*. But at least he was talking, just when he was sure his throat was as dry as a desert. Mr Richardson, though, didn't appear to be critical of him; smiling effortlessly, he introduced another, younger, man, whom he described as "your" producer. The "your" bit was, James guessed, intended to give his ego a boost: and it did. The younger man, Claudio, just nodded at James and fine-tuned some equipment on the far side of the room where a large-screen TV set dominated the wall.

"We're going to run a video for you," Mr Richardson explained. "I'm sure you'll recognize the teams and know most of the players. You may even have been at the match yourself, James. We'll run it through first to give you a chance to get the feel of the action. Then, second time round, I'd like you to give us a commentary on what you see: just describe the action and tell us, the *listeners*, anything you think is relevant. Don't overdo it. Most viewers can follow the main direction of the play for themselves, so they don't want *everything* spelled out for them. OK?"

James nodded, momentarily unwilling to trust his voice. The next few minutes, he realized, could be the most important of his life. His future career could be decided before he left this nerve-racking room. To his delight, however, the teams turned out to be Arsenal and Liverpool and their players were almost as familiar to him as his school-mates. The match, he recalled, was the previous season's Charity Shield at Wembley and he'd actually watched the highlights on TV that night. He might even be able to remember striking phrases. Perhaps, though, he should avoid that because if they knew them, Mr Richardson and Claudio might feel he was completely unoriginal.

"I, er, might not recognize everyone," he pointed out in another sudden loss of confidence.

"Doesn't matter a bit," the genial Mr Richardson assured him. "This is not a memory test, either – not at this stage, anyway. Plenty of opportunities to test your powers of recall later, James.

No, what we're interested in at present is your fluency and style and confidence. They're really what matter, you see." He paused, smiled invitingly and added: "Right, Mr Commentator, we're ready when you are. Just move into the action and tell us what's going on out there. Just talk us through it."

The pictures came back on the screen and James, after clearing his throat a couple of times and fingering his throat mike to make sure it was still in place, launched into a commentary. He knew at once that he was going too fast but felt powerless to slow down. It was as if an irresistible current was carrying him towards a distant land and only when he reached it would he feel safe again. Twice he stumbled over the name of a Mexican defender, twice he corrected himself with anxious glances at his producer, who appeared to be interested only in the screen, and twice he had to clear his throat again when mysteriously the phrase he wanted eluded him.

Then: "And Jones, Jones has the ball, he's swerving, *weaving*, his way into the penalty area – and he hots a shot – oh, sorry, *hits* a, a shot and . . ."

His voice trailed away as he worried about his awful error. Mr Richardson, however, appeared unconcerned and simply made a rolling-over motion with his hand to indicate that James should keep going.

But James couldn't resume. He licked his lips, swallowed deeply, tried to *force* the words out; but they wouldn't come. Someone had once forecast that "James will never be tongue-tied" and he'd laughed with pleasure. Now he experienced what it must be like to have your tongue literally tied down, like a horse that might swallow its tongue in a race. Then, when at last he could croak out a word, it was another apology.

"Don't *worry*," Mr Richardson tried to reassure him. "Many people get their vowels in a twist," he added, his eyes sparkling. "It could have been worse in this case. At least you got the 'shot' bit right! OK, son, try again."

It was hopeless. Another few phrases stuttered out, for a moment or two he even kept pace with the action, but whatever rhythm was needed he couldn't find it. He knew he sounded as

fluent and interesting as a dying parrot. For the first time since entering the studio he sat back in his seat; then he spread his arms wide in surrender and murmured: "Sorry, I'm really sorry!"

Claudio switched the video off. Mr Richardson stood up, lips pursed and gave a quick, sad shake of his head. "I'm sorry, too, son, but we both know it's not working out. I think maybe you're lacking in real confidence at the moment. This job is all in the mind, really. If you have confidence in yourself and what you're doing or saying, well, then the listener is on your side."

He paused fractionally before continuing: "But if you sound hesitant, uncertain, you've lost your audience completely. But you're young enough to put it all together one of these days. Just keep practising, and not just on your own, either. Make sure you have at least one person listening. A small crowd's best, people who can watch as well as listen. As the words flow, the confidence will grow! Now, can we help with any expenses you might have run up getting here?"

James shook his head. He knew he was being dismissed and still he couldn't open his mouth to say the right thing. Partly, he knew, it must be because he'd blown it and so there was nothing to say. Would he ever get a second chance? That was all that mattered now.

"Look, son, we'll keep your name and phone number on file in case we run anything like this again. Or in case our top radio man wins the pools and stops working for a living," Mr Richardson said cheerfully.

"Thanks," James managed to say, and was genuinely thankful that his voice had returned. Now he knew the real meaning behind that jokey phrase his parents sometimes used about rejections: don't call us, we'll call you. As he made his way out of the studio and down the depressing stairs he tried to think what to say to his mates, the ones who knew he was entering what he'd described as a competition. They did not know the test was tonight but they'd find out somehow. There was always somebody at school who unearthed the facts that others preferred to hide. Still, he thought he'd stall about it as long as possible.

Home was unthinkable at the moment and he reduced the alternatives to the library: there he could consider his future and be confident no one would interrupt him if he buried himself in a book.

It hadn't occurred to him that he might meet someone he knew before he reached the sheltering shelves. But sitting at one of the tables, studying a magazine about engineering, was Xavier, who'd once declared he was going to be a bridge builder; and Xavier looked up just as James tip-toed past him. Xavier grinned wickedly and said in a stage whisper: "They won't let you do soccer commentaries in here, you know. Silence rules!"

James managed not to be too embarrassed. "I'm just here to check some facts, that's all," he said softly. Xavier nodded as if he believed him and then returned to the riveting details of his construction article. So James was free to move away and hide himself behind a stack, his eyes on a page but taking nothing in. He wasn't even aware of when Xavier departed. When he himself left the library it was late and he thought he was safe from interrogation.

The first question at school next morning was staggering. "So how'd you get on, then?" Peter Colne inquired eagerly. "At the studio?" James tried to swallow his dismay: how in this world did they find out? He fenced but Peter stabbed through his feeble guard. "Look, my sister works there, she's the stand-in receptionist or whatever they call it. Told me when she came home that a boy from school had been there. Told me everything when I asked. Fiona's dead keen to tell everybody what a great job she's doing now and how the manager's dead impressed with her. So, give, James, give."

"Er, well, we, I don't know, not really," he floundered, his usual fluency deserting him again. "You see, it wasn't a proper competition, just a sort of trial, so well, there's nothing to report, Peter. I mean, if they want me back again for another test they'll let me know."

It was the best he could think of and he was aware of the interest fading from the other boy's grey-blue eyes; they were about to resume their customary coolness. "But I got the idea that the opposition was, well, a bit hot," he added as an excuse he hoped could be accepted.

Peter nodded. "Fiona said you left looking a bit glum. I thought you might just have been lost in your own thoughts. You often are when you're dreaming up one of your match commentaries."

After that, no one mentioned his failure to him personally, though he suspected the ones who used to form his old audiences, the ones who hung on every descriptive word and urged him on to greater heights, talked about it behind his back. By then he was yesterday's news and some other performer or temporary hero was in the spotlight. So James abandoned his public performances while continuing to practise his skills and add to his soccer knowledge at home in his own room or when he was absolutely certain he was alone on the cliffs or the beach or the supermarket car park on Sunday mornings. The BBC didn't telephone him and within a month he'd given up the idea they ever would.

So when, one Sunday evening, the phone did ring and his mother said someone called Sue Hardy was asking for him he couldn't imagine what it might be about. The name was unknown to him and, reluctant to speak to a complete stranger, he was hesitant about even picking up the receiver.

"James, you're the boy who does football commentaries, aren't you?" a voice asked without any preliminaries. "Well, I'd like you to do one for me, for my family, really. Will you help us, please?"

Not for the first time in recent weeks, he was lost for words. "Er, sorry," he stumbled at last, "I don't understand."

"No, of course not, I've not explained myself at all and—"

"Listen, I'm not being set up, am I?" James cut in fiercely, suddenly guessing what might be going on. "My mates at school have fixed this, haven't they? Just for a laugh, right?"

"I only wish it were a laughing matter, James, believe me. But this is completely serious," replied the calm, clear voice. "It's deadly serious, in fact, a matter of life and death. Yes, it's exactly that – a matter of life and death."

She paused, as if awaiting a comment, but James, not knowing how to respond now, said nothing. So she continued: "Let me just briefly explain our problem and then you can tell me if you're willing to help. You must have time to think about it before you decide but for the moment I just want to put you in the picture. Is that all right with you, James?"

"Oh yes, yes, of course," he answered while wondering what on earth he was going to hear next. The sincerity in her voice was now unmissable.

"I'll be as brief as I can because I hope we're going to meet very soon when I can explain things in greater detail," she resumed. "This is what it's about, James. I have a son, Neil, who is just about your age and just as passionate about football as you are. I learned this from a boy who's at school with you. He's called Xavier and he lives near us and is a good friend of Neil's. Well, almost five weeks ago, thirty-three days ago to be exact because I'll never forget that day, Neil was knocked off his bike by a car and knocked unconscious. He hasn't woken up yet. The doctors say there is no reason why he shouldn't wake up at any time. Perhaps he just needs the right stimulus."

Her pause this time was too brief for James to speak. She went on: "We spend all the time that's possible sitting with him, talking, talking, talking. Hoping desperately that he'll respond to a voice or a sound – we play music as well. All sorts of things – anything – *anything* that might work. Football is what he loves most. He simply idolizes Arsenal and all their players. One of them has actually been to sit with Neil and try to chat with him. Unfortunately, it didn't work. Nothing happened and I think the player felt a bit, well, uncomfortable. But it was wonderful of him to make the effort.

"James, this is what we think. If you'd be prepared to sit with him and make up commentaries about Arsenal matches or something like that then there must be a chance he'll respond. You're his age, as I said, so your kind of voice will be familiar to him. It could work. Oh, and I must tell you one other thing to reassure you because people worry about what they might find when they go into a hospital. Neil looks perfectly normal. He's not been disfigured in any way. He did have to have his hair

136

shaved off so that a head injury could be attended to but it's growing back very well. So when you see him he'll just look as if he's fast asleep. So, James, it should not be an ordeal. Now, having heard all that, will you help us, will you try to help him?"

"Yes," he answered without any hesitation at all. "Yes, I'd like to, very much."

On previous visits, not much seemed to have changed. The silent patient was always hooked up to the machine that monitored his heart beat and his breathing and showed the results with a flickering blue line on a screen; and he was still being fed by the ominous-looking plastic tube that led to a vein in his arm. Even the level of orange juice in the bottle for the use of visitors appeared unchanged.

On this Sunday morning, though, something was different. "You'll notice a sort of low hum when you get into his room, James," said Nurse Bernadette, casually meeting him as he turned into the corridor that was as long as a football pitch. "Don't worry about it. Nothing to alarm anybody. Y'see it's from the power unit for his new ripple bed. Ingenious it is. The bed moves to prevent the pressure problems caused when somebody lies in the same spot for hours without moving. So it's really good for nurses as well as patients."

James nodded his understanding. He felt now that he knew a lot about hospitals, the people who worked there and medical techniques. "But Neil won't know anything about that yet, will he?" he remarked with a smile.

"Indeed he won't. No change in him at all, I'm afraid. But we're not giving up hope, are we? One day or night . . ."

She went off briskly, her smile switching from sad to cheerful because nurses are not supposed to appear downcast to patients or strangers. Later, James knew, she would drop in with a cup of coffee for him as he sat and talked to Neil. Sunday mornings were usually fairly quiet in this hospital as most of the patients did not have visitors then. James felt privileged not only to be admitted but made so welcome.

"Hi, Neil, it's me again, your old football mate, James Boston," he sang out as he entered the room Neil occupied on his own. "Hope you're ready for a terrific commentary on Arsenal's victory yesterday over those great rivals of yours. Yeah, that's right, Spurs! So, fantastic result, right! Worth six points, not just the usual old three."

Neil looked just as relaxed and normal as ever. The first time James had seen him his hair was still short but now it really needed cutting. From time to time James thought he detected the faintest fluttering of the eyelids but then he supposed he was imagining things; at first he'd been desperate to get a response to his attempts at communication and so he stared intently at the patient, willing him to give *some* sign that he could hear. But it never happened.

Settling himself into the surprisingly comfortable chair to the left of the bed, he made the snap decision to start with a description of Arsenal's winning goal instead of providing his hoped-for listener with a conventional build-up. Perhaps the suddenness of the excitement might trigger off a response. But it didn't. Within seconds he reached a crescendo of drama before the ball "ripped into the back of the net. And Arsenal have scored, they've hit what could be the WINNER!" Though James quite enjoyed his own commentary it all too plainly had served no purpose. His voice faded away and he fell silent. What could he try next? His imagination failed him completely.

He thought of Neil's parents and what it must be like for them, day after day without a glimmer of improvement. They had, as they told him at their first meeting on the hospital steps, tried every trick anyone could think of, from playing pop songs at full volume to whispering family jokes into one ear and then the other. The doctors said there was no reason so far as they could tell why he couldn't wake at any time: but only when he regained consciousness and responded to them would it be known whether he'd suffered any brain damage.

"Still dreaming?" Bernadette inquired brightly, popping in with his customary cup of coffee.

"Still dreaming," he replied, sharing their sympathetic shorthand for Neil's condition.

And he was still occupying his own world when James, his spirits low again, left very nearly an hour later. All he could hope was that Neil's parents and sister would achieve the breakthrough when they turned up that afternoon. He kept thinking of Neil's eyelids: so thin they seemed almost to be transparent, hiding blue eyes – and so much else. If only, if only they'd open . . . if only Neil Hardy would come back to the real world.

James found that he was thinking about him much of the time when talking football with his mates (for whom he still did the occasional commentary when he was in the mood or they demanded one). He thought about Neil when he was with his family, doing something as ordinary as arguing over a meal, or which TV programme to watch. He thought about Neil when he was riding his bike to the shops or across an intersection on the southern bypass. That's where Neil had been sent crashing to the ground by a reckless motorist who hadn't even stopped afterwards. "He just mowed Neil down like a, a *maniac* tackling someone on a football field. Neil could be as daft as any boy his age – sorry, James! – but this was one time when he did nothing wrong. It really was the other guy." That was how Mrs Hardy described it to him at their first meeting and James found the words were frozen into his mind.

"Any change?" his mother asked with genuine interest when he arrived home. James was aware that his family were as desperate to hear good news as he was. He shook his head.

"I do admire you for keeping this up, James," she said, and he knew she meant it. "But – but – it does seem hopeless, doesn't it? I mean, no one would blame you if you felt like giving up these visits. They must be an ordeal."

"I like to go and see him, so it's not an ordeal, not really," he tried to assure her. "I mean, I know it seems as if I'm not getting anywhere but, well, who knows? Everybody else keeps hoping, so I must, too."

All the same, he didn't really believe anything was going to be any different when he returned to the hospital the following Friday evening, a time when Mr and Mrs Hardy couldn't be present. Nurse Bernadette was actually the first person he saw, carrying a cloth-covered tray, but she was hurrying down a corridor and had time only to give him a big wink and a "Hi, James." Neil looked exactly as he always did and the only change in the room appeared to be a vase of chrysanthemums. Somebody had brought in fresh flowers again and James supposed at least the visitors enjoyed looking at them.

That afternoon he'd been playing football himself at school and was still feeling twinges of discomfort from a crunching tackle that had caught him just above the ankle. He wasn't going to reflect on his failure to wear the shinpads the PE staff tried to insist on for every player. Now he massaged the tender area and tried to decide what to tell Neil about tonight. But he couldn't think of anything different or exciting as he attempted to rub the pain away in his leg. Then, suddenly, it occurred to him to dramatize the incident in which he'd been injured: let Neil hear about a fellow-sufferer. Well, not quite in the same league, but . . .

"And here we are, watching this game between the Superstars of the Third Years of Kettlesing School and the, er, well, to be honest, we have to describe them as the No-Hopers. Same age but very different skills – in fact, not much skill at all, really," James began tentatively, trying to strike the right note and get a good rhythm to his narrative. "And now the ball's swung over to the left wing by Stephens, that, er, hard-working midfielder. He's trying to find James Boston, a tricky, alert winger and Boston sprints to take the pass – he's got possession and – oh, NO! Boston's gone down under a, a *ferocious* tackle from Middleton. CRASH! Midders went in like a load of rubble and Boston, well, Boston's plainly hurt. Not surprisingly after a bludgeoning tackle like that and . . ."

James stopped. The words vanished from his brain. Until a moment earlier he hadn't actually been looking at Neil. In his mind he'd been seeing the field of play, not the boy on the bed. Now, as he looked with widening eyes, he saw that Neil's eyelids were fluttering. Then there seemed to be a sharp, spastic movement of the left hand. And then Neil said something – or

140

tried to say something. There was a sound, definitely a sound. Though whether it was a word or just a syllable or another noise James had no idea. His heart began to pound as it would if he were about to take a penalty kick or watch the climax of a gripping film.

For some moments he couldn't move at all. All he could do was watch what was happening to the boy who'd been in a coma for weeks. Then James knew without any doubt at all that the coma was coming to an end.

He'd been told what to do if that happened and now he did it. Leaping to the door, he opened it, looked out and called urgently: "Nurse, nurse!" No one he knew was about so he hurried down the corridor, desperate to find someone. Then the second miracle in moments occurred: Bernadette turned into the corridor at the far end, heading towards him with a cup of coffee.

"He's waking up, he IS! I'm sure of it. Come and—"

"No!" she said authoritatively. Then she spoke rapidly into a personal phone before switching back to James. "I'll go, but you must go to the waiting-room, James. That's the rule. You can't stay with a patient in such a situation. I've sent for the doctor. If you're right, the doctor will have lots to do. Off you go – and I'll let you know the news as soon as I can. Oh, and well done. Here, you deserve this."

She thrust the hot cup into his hands and ran to Neil's room.

Somehow he managed to carry the cup all the way to the waiting-room without spilling a drop. He didn't think he could sit still for a moment however long he had to wait for the news. His memory came to his aid for he recalled a scene from an old film where an expectant father paced up and down, up and down, while his wife gave birth in the next room. Now James could share the man's sense of disbelief and wonder and the urgent need for confirmation that all was going to be all right.

Then, later, but how much later he never knew, it was Neil's mother who came bursting into the room. He was just able to see the tears of joy before she flung her arms around him and hugged him harder than he'd ever been hugged in his life. He couldn't find the breath even to speak.

"Oh, James, thank you, thank you, thank you!" she cried at last as she released him and stepped back for a moment. "I can hardly believe you've done it, but you have, you have! You've talked him through it! He's come out of his lost world. The doctor says it'll not all change at once but he says there's no reason on earth why Neil shouldn't make a full recovery."

And now that he had the breath to speak James didn't know what to say. He wished he could tell her that he'd never experienced a happier moment in his entire life. Because that was the truth.

"So, James, my dearest James," she added in a voice that was scarcely above a whisper, "thank God for football and for you and for everyone else who truly loves that game."

CLIFFHANGER

JACQUELINE WILSON

Cliffhanger *is packed with entertaining sporting action – ranging from adventure-style sports such as climbing, abseiling and canoeing to more informal activities, including a highly competitive team obstacle race, which is described here. The book's central character Tim is hopeless at sports of any kind – or so he believes. But as this extract shows, in sport a good brain can be every bit as important as physical prowess.*

Jake and Sally had set this huge great obstacle race. We were all lined up in our teams: the Lions, the Panthers, the Cheetahs – and us. Giles was dead eager. Kelly was bobbing about, Theresa clutched in her fist. Laura and Lesley were giggling. Biscuits and I were *groaning*.

"It's not my idea of fun," I whispered.

"You can say that again," Biscuits whispered back.

We kept this up all the time Sally was explaining what we had to do. It involved a lot of running. Lots and lots of running.

We had to run to the paddling pool and fill our buckets with water and then we had to run – with the full buckets – all the way round the field to the slide and then – still with the buckets – we had to climb up it and slide down and *then* we had to run to the sandpit and stagger across – with the buckets – and THEN we had to run to the stream and at the other side of the water there were four thirsty baby big cats desperate for a bucketful of water. Well, that's what Sally said.

"Can you go through it again, Sally? I wasn't concentrating," said Biscuits, grinning.

Sally pretended to clip him over the ear.

Giles was dead set on getting the rules right.

"So it's the team that fills the painted rubbish bin first that wins, yes?"

"They're not bins, Giles, they're babies. A baby lion, a baby panther, a baby cheetah, and *we've* got a baby tiger," said Kelly. "Doesn't it look sweet?"

Giles screwed up his face in disgust at this whimsy.

I thought the bins looked good. The Baby Lion bin was painted yellow, the Baby Panther bin was painted black, the Baby Cheetah bin was painted beige with black spots, and our Baby Tiger bin looked the best, painted orange with black stripes. They all had cardboard ears and beady eyes and the swingtops made excellent movable mouths. Jake demonstrated, making them open their mouths to pant for water.

Jake jumped over the stream to get to them. He's got long legs but it was still quite a stretch for him. And he wasn't carrying a bucket of water. But there were four drainpipes across the stream. It looked as if we were in for a very wobbly walk across.

"And the team that fills the bin first wins?" Giles repeated impatiently, raring to go.

"Not so fast, pal," said Sally. "The first team gets forty points, the second team gets thirty, the third team gets twenty. The last team only gets ten points."

"Guess who's going to be last," I muttered to Biscuits.

"But the Crazy Bucket race isn't just about coming first," said Sally, smiling. "We measure how much water is in each of the bins. That's just as important. You get forty points if your bin is the fullest. Then thirty, then twenty, then ten."

"It's starting to sound like a maths lesson," said Lesley. "I can't get the hang of it, can you, Laura?"

"It's all much simpler than it sounds," said Sally. "Cheer up. It's fun!"

Biscuits pulled a silly face at me. I pulled one back. Giles pushed us into place.

"Come on, you lot, stop messing about. We're going to win, right?"

"Wrong!"

"Look, *try*," said Giles.

"My dad always tells me to try," I told Biscuits. "And I do. But it doesn't work."

"Right everyone," Sally called. "Get ready. One. Two. Three. GO!"

We all started running. Guess what. Giles got to the pool first.

"Come *on*, you Tigers!" he bawled as he filled his bucket.

Biscuits and I were nearly last at the pool. We filled our buckets right to the brim. We certainly weren't going to fill our baby big cat bin first, so we knew we had to bring our entire bucketful.

It was hard going, running with a full bucket. We had to be ever so careful not to spill any. Some of the faster kids swung their buckets and sprinkled water all down their socks. Biscuits didn't spill any, but he was slower than ever. I jogged along beside him, proud that I hadn't spilled a single drop.

And then one of the Cheetahs pushed past me, his bucket banging hard into my back. I staggered and fell headlong, spilling all the water in my bucket.

"Ooooh!" All the breath was knocked out of me.

"Oh Tim!" said Biscuits, ever so upset. "That Cheetah pushed into you on purpose. He really *did* cheat!"

Giles was yelling at me from a long way off.

"Tim! You're so *useless!*"

I lay there, still juddering. I had my eyes shut because I was trying very hard not to cry.

"You cheaty old Cheetah!" I heard Kelly bellow.

There was a yell and a thump and a splash. When I opened my eyes I saw the Cheetah sprawling on the ground, soaking wet, Kelly standing over him triumphantly.

"Hey! Hey! You'll all end up disqualified if you're not careful!" Jake called. "Is Tim OK?"

I wasn't sure. There was wet on my knees. It wasn't just the water from my bucket. I was *bleeding*.

"Maybe you'd better go and get them bandaged?" said Biscuits.

I stood up very slowly. The blood spurted a bit more. I had a truly great excuse to get out of finishing the race.

I looked at Biscuits. I looked at Kelly. I looked at Laura and Lesley, who were running back to see if I was all right. I looked at Giles. He was yelling again.

"Come *on*! We've all got to finish. You can't let us down, Tim!"

I didn't mind letting Giles down *at all*. But I didn't want to spoil it for the others.

"I'm OK," I said. "I'll run back to fill my bucket again."

"We'll wait for you," said Biscuits.

"No, I'll catch you up."

So I ran all the way back to the pool, even though my knees were hurting quite badly. Then I filled my bucket and started the long run again, way way way behind all the others, though two Lions then bumped into each other and had to go back to the pool as well. And more came a cropper on the slide. There was a whole bunch who fought to go first and spilled all their water. By the time *I* got to the slide it was clear and I could take it slowly. I didn't spill a drop.

I caught Biscuits up at the sandpit. We staggered through the sand, balancing our buckets.

"It's like being at the seaside," I said.

"I couldn't half do with an ice cream," said Biscuits longingly. "Or an ice-lolly. Or a can of cola. No, a bottle of Tizer. Or an ice-cream soda. No, better, a Knickerbocker Glory . . ."

He was off in a wistful food fantasy right up until we got to the stream. Jake was swinging the bin mouths again.

"They're so *thirsty*," Jake called. "They're desperate. Water, water!"

But we were all the other side of the stream with our buckets. None of the others had made it across. Some of the children were very wet, after several attempts.

"Let me have a go," said Kelly, elbowing Giles and Laura and Lesley out of the way.

146

She started edging along the wobbly drainpipe, holding her bucket out. The drainpipe was only lightly wedged into the ground at either side of the stream. It jiggled at each step. Kelly wobbled, but got halfway across. She turned round to make sure we were watching her. She wobbled again, lost her balance, slipped off the drainpipe and fell into the stream. She had the presence of mind to clutch her bucket to her chest so that it didn't *all* spill. She added a bit of stream water for luck when she thought Jake wasn't watching.

"Hey, Kelly, no sly refilling that bucket!" he shouted. "Empty half of that out."

Kelly sighed and muttered but did as she was told.

"*I'll* have a go," said Giles. "I'll have a little practice without my bucket."

He made it halfway across too. Then the drainpipe jiggled and Giles wobbled and he went flying too. He made a leap for it so that he didn't get totally soaked like Kelly. He just got water all down his trouser legs.

"You look like you've wet yourself Giles," said Laura, and she and Lesley fell about laughing.

"Come on!" Jake urged from the other side of the bank. "Think of a way to give these babies a proper drink."

Kelly was peeling her sodden shoes and socks off.

"Hey, why don't we just paddle across?" she said. "I'm sure it's shallow enough."

"Not allowed," said Jake, and he picked up a log and threw it in the stream. "See that log? It's *really* a crocodile. You paddle, he'll come along and enjoy a leg sandwich."

"Well, it's easier without shoes and socks on anyway," said Kelly, having another go across the drainpipe.

She ran to show how easy it was. She slipped and fell in again.

"Whoops," said Kelly, clambering up the bank. "*Slightly* easier." She shook herself like a wet dog and then dug Theresa out of her pocket and gave her a squeeze too. "We're not too keen on this swimming lark, are we, Theresa?"

"This is stupid," said Laura. "It's too difficult, Jake. It's all right for you. You can jump across."

"I bet *I* could jump across," said Giles. "Look. Watch me."

He took several giant steps backwards, revved up, hurtled forward, leapt into space and soared over the stream. He staggered a bit when he landed in the mud at the other side, but he'd made it. He punched the air triumphantly, thrilled with himself.

"But you haven't got your bucket," said Kelly.

The Cheetahs were watching. Their tallest boy tried leaping the stream with his bucket. He made it to the other side. But most of the water sprayed out of his bucket as he leapt. Lots of the others had a go. Without success.

"They're s-o-o-o-o thirsty, these baby big cats," said Jake. "Try harder!"

"We are jolly well trying," said Kelly.

"Think of a way of giving them their drink," said Jake.

"Well we've all tried to get across," said Kelly. "Apart from Biscuits and Tim." She looked at us hopefully.

"You've got to be joking!" Giles called from the other side of the stream. "If Fatso stands on the drainpipe, he'll bust it in two."

"I'll bust you in two in a minute, Piles," said Biscuits.

"Tim?" said Kelly.

"There's even less point asking him," said Giles.

I was thinking. It was like a puzzle game. We were all trying to do it the hard way. There had to be an *easy* way . . .

I suddenly had an idea. Though I wasn't sure if it would be allowed.

"Well," I started.

But they were all watching one of the Lion girls who had balanced her way right along the drainpipe. She was almost at the end. But then she suddenly wobbled – and went.

"Oooh!" said everyone.

"See. *No one* can do it, Jake," said Laura, getting cross.

Jake just laughed at her.

"Did you have an idea, Tim?" he called.

"*He* won't be able to do it," said Laura. "He fell over just on the field."

"You try walking the drainpipe, Laura, I'm sure you could do it," said Lesley.

"If you can get the bucket three quarter of the way over then I can reach across and get it," said Giles.

"But you don't have to do it that way," I said.

"You shut up, Tim," Giles shouted.

I'd suddenly had enough of being shouted at. And I really did have a good idea.

"No, *you* shut up, Giles," I yelled. "Pick your end of the drainpipe up and stick it in the baby tiger's mouth."

Giles stared at me, going, "You what?"

But Jake jumped up and down and gave me the thumbs-up sign. I'd cracked it!

"Kelly and Biscuits, you hold the drainpipe this end," I said, telling them what to do. "Laura and Lesley, pass me the buckets. Look!"

It was so *simple*. We didn't have to walk across the stream on the drainpipes. They were hollow inside, like giant straws. We could empty the water down the drainpipe right into the Baby Tiger bin.

And that's exactly what we did.

"Well done, Tim!" Jake shouted.

"Oh, Tim! Brilliant!" said Kelly, giving me a hug. "You're so clever."

"Super-Tim," said Biscuits.

"Why didn't we think if it," said Laura.

"Look, everyone's copying us now!" said Lesley.

"But *we've* won!" said Giles, capering about. "We're first to fill the bin – and we've got it nearly full to the top too. We've *won*! Hurray for Tim!"

All the Tigers jumped up and down and cheered. Cheering me. And I jumped up and down and cheered me too!

FEET

JAN MARK

UNLIKE THE CENTRE COURT AT WIMBLEDON, the Centre Court at our school is the one nobody wants to play on. It is made of asphalt and has dents in it, like Ryvita. All the other courts are grass, out in the sun; Centre Court is in between the science block and the canteen and when there is a Governors' Meeting the governors use it as a car park. The sun only shines on Centre Court at noon in June and there is green algae growing round the edges. When I volunteered to be an umpire at the annual tennis tournament I might have known that I was going to end up on Centre Court.

"You'd better go on Centre Court," said Mr Evans, "as it's your first time. It won't matter so much if you make mistakes." I love Mr Evans. He is so tactful and he looks like an orang-utan in his track suit. I believe myself that he swings from the pipes in the changing room but I haven't personally observed this, you understand.

He just looks as if he might enjoy swinging from things. He has very long arms. Probably he can peel bananas with his toes, which have little tufts of hair on, like beard transplants. I saw them once.

So I was sitting up in my umpire's chair, just like Wimbledon, with an official school pencil and a pad of score cards and I wasn't making any mistakes. This was mainly because they were all first-round matches, the 6–0, 6–0 kind, to get rid of the worst players. All my matches were ladies' doubles which is what you call the fifth- and sixth-year girls when they are playing tennis although not at any other time. We didn't get any spectators except some first-year boys who came to look at the legs and things and Mr Evans, on and off, who was probably there for the same reason.

All the men's matches were on the grass courts, naturally, so I didn't see anything I wanted to see which was Michael Collier. I suppose it was the thought of umpiring Collier that made me put my name down in the first place, before I remembered about ending up on Centre Court. I could only hope that I would be finished in time for the Men's Final so that I could go and watch it because definitely Collier would be in the final. People said that it was hardly worth his while playing, really, why didn't they just give him the trophy and have done with it?

Looking back, I dare say that's what he thought, too.

So anyway, I got rid of all my ladies' doubles and sat around waiting for a mixed doubles. It was cold and windy on Centre Court since it wasn't noon in June, and I wished I had worn a sweater instead of trying to look attractive sort of in short sleeves. Sort of is right. That kind of thing doesn't fool anyone. I had these sandals too which let the draught in something rotten. I should have worn wellies. No one would have noticed. Nobody looks at feet.

After the mixed doubles which was a fiasco I thought of going in to get a hot drink – tea or coffee or just boiling water would have done – when I noticed this thing coming down the tramlines and trying to walk on one leg like Richard the Third only all in white.

Richard the Bride.

It was using a tennis racquet head-down as a walking stick which is not done, like cheating at cards. No gentleman would do this to his tennis racquet. This is no gentleman.

"Ho," says this Richard the Third person. "Me Carson. You Jane."

This does not quite qualify as Pun of the Week because he *is* Carson and I *am* Jane. He is Alan Carson from the sixth form – only he is at Oxford now and he would not know me from Adam only he is a neighbour and used to baby-sit with me once. This is humiliating and I don't tell people.

Carson is known to do a number of strange things and walking on one leg may be one of them for all I know so I do not remark on it.

"Hello, Carson," I said, very coolly. I was past sounding warm, anyway. "Where are you going?"

Carson sits down on a stacking chair at the foot of my ladder.

"I'm going to get changed," he says.

"Did you lose your match?" I say, tactfully like Mr Evans. (I am surprised because he is next most likely after Collier to be in the final.)

"No, I won," says Carson. "But it was a Pyrrhic victory," and he starts whanging the net post with his tennis racquet, boing boing. (This is not good for it either, I should think.)

I have heard about Pyrrhic victories but I do not know what they are.

"What's a Pyrrhic victory?" I said.

"One you can do without," said Carson. "Named after King Pyrrhus of Epirus who remarked, after beating the Romans in a battle, 'One more win like this and we've had it,' on account of the Romans badly chewing up his army."

"Oh," I said. "And did he get another win?"

"Yes," said Carson. "But then he got done over at the battle Beneventum by Curius Dentatus the famous Roman General with funny teeth. Now I just knocked spots off Pete Baldwin in the quarter-final and I'm running up to the net to thank him for a jolly good game old boy, when I turn my ankle and fall flat on my back. It's a good thing," he added, thoughtfully, "that I didn't get as far as the net, because I should have jumped over it and *then* fallen flat on my back."

I could see his point. That's the kind of thing that happens to me.

"I should have met Mick Collier in the semi-final," said

Carson. "Now he'll have a walk-over. Which should suit him. He doesn't care where he puts his feet."

"Who will play in the final?" I say, terribly pleased for Collier as well as being sorry for Carson whose ankle is definitely swelling as even I can see without my glasses which I do not wear in between matches although everyone can see I wear them because of the red mark across my nose.

"Mills or McGarrity," says Carson. "Mills is currently beating McGarrity and then Collier will beat Mills to pulp – and no one will be surprised. I don't know why we bother," he says, tiredly. "It was a foregone conclusion," and he limps away, dragging his injured foot and not even trying to be funny about it because obviously it hurts like hell.

Then it started to rain.

Everybody came and sheltered in the canteen and griped, especially Mills and McGarrity, especially Mills who was within an inch of winning and wanted to get that over and have a crack at Collier who was a more worthy opponent. McGarrity heard all this and looked as if he would like to give Mills a dead leg – or possibly a dead head.

Then it stops raining and Mr Evans the games master and Miss Sylvia Truman who is our lady games master go out and skid about on the grass courts to see if they are safe. They are not. Even then I do not realize what is going to happen because Collier comes over to the dark corner where I am skulking with my cold spotty arms and starts talking to *me*!

"Jane Turner, isn't it?" he says. He must have asked somebody because he couldn't possibly know otherwise. I was only a fourth year then.

And I say, "Yes."

And he says, "I see you every day on the bus, don't I?"

And I say, "Yes," although I travel downstairs and he travels up, among the smokers although of course he doesn't smoke himself because of his athlete's lungs.

And he says, "You're an umpire today, aren't you?"

And I say "Yes."

And he says, "Do you play?"

And I say "Yes," which I do and not badly but I don't go in for tournaments because people watch and if I was being watched I would foul it up.

"We have a court at home," he says which I know because he is a near neighbour like Carson although me and Carson live on the Glebelands Estate and the Colliers live in the Old Rectory. And then he says, *"You ought to come over and play, sometime."*

And I can't believe this but I say, "Yes. Yes please. Yes, I'd like that." And I still don't believe it.

And he says, "Bring your cousin and make up a foursome. That was your cousin who was sitting next to you, wasn't it, on the bus?" and I know he must have been asking about me because my cousin Dawn is only staying with us for a week.

And I say, "Yes," and he says, "Come on Friday, then," and I say, "Yes." Again. And I wonder how I can last out till Friday evening. It is only three-fifteen on Wednesday.

And then Mr Evans and Miss Sylvia Truman come in from skidding about and Mr Evans, finalist in the All-England Anthropoid Ape Championship says, "The grass is kaput. We'll have to finish up on Centre Court. Come on Collier. Come on Mills," and McGarrity says, "Mills hasn't beaten me yet, Sir," and Sir says, "Oh, well," and doesn't say, "It's a foregone conclusion," and Miss Sylvia Truman says, "Well hurry up and finish him off, Mills," in a voice that McGarrity isn't supposed to hear but does.

(If Miss Sylvia Truman *was* a man instead of just looking like one, McGarrity would take her apart, but doesn't, because she isn't. Also, she is much bigger than McGarrity.)

And Sir says, "Where's the umpire?" and I say, "Here I am," and Sir says, "Can you manage?" and I say, "I haven't made any mistakes yet."

"But it's the *final*," says Fiery Fred Truman who thinks I am an imbecile – I have heard her – but I say I can manage and I am desperate to do it because of Collier playing and perhaps Sir has been fortifying himself with the flat bottle he thinks we don't know about but which we can see the outline of in his hip pocket, because he says, "All right, Jane," and I can't believe it.

But anyway, we all go out to the damp green canyon that is Centre Court and I go up my ladder and Mills finishes off McGarrity love, love, love, love, and still I don't make any mistakes.

And then suddenly *everybody* is there to watch because it is Mills versus Collier and we all want/know that Collier will win.

Collier comes and takes off his sweater and hangs it on the rung of my chair and says, "Don't be too hard on me, Jane," with that smile that would make you love him even if you didn't like him, and I say, "I've got to be impartial," and he smiles and I wish that I didn't have to be impartial and I am afraid that I won't be impartial.

He says, "I won't hold it against you, Jane." And he says, "Don't forget Friday."

I say, "I won't forget Friday," as loudly as I can so that as many people as possible will hear, which they do.

You can see them being surprised all round the court.

"And don't forget your cousin," he says, and I say, "Oh, she's going home on Thursday morning."

"Some other time, then," he says.

"No, no," I said. "*I* can come on Friday," but he was already walking on to the court and he just looked over his shoulder and said, "No, it doesn't matter," and all round the court you could see people not being surprised. And I was up there on that lousy stinking ladder and *everybody* could see me.

I thought I was going to cry and spent a long time putting my glasses on. Collier and Mills began to knock-up and I got out the pencil and the score cards and broke the point off the pencil. I didn't have another one and I didn't want to show my face asking anybody to lend me one so I had to bite the wood away from the lead and of course it didn't have a proper point and made two lines instead of one. And gritty.

And then I remembered that I had to start them off so I said, "Play, please. Collier to serve." He had won the toss. Naturally.

My voice had gone woolly and my glasses had steamed over and I was sure people were laughing, even if they weren't. Then I heard this voice down by my feet saying, "Let him get on with it.

156

If he won't play with you on Friday he can play with himself," which kind of remark would normally make me go red only I was red already. I looked down and there was Carson looking not at all well because of his foot, probably, but he gave me an evil wink and I remembered that he was a very kind person, really. I remembered that he sometimes gave me a glass of beer when he was baby-sitting. (I was only eleven, then, when he baby-sat. My mother was fussy about leaving us and there was my baby brother as well. He wasn't really sitting with *me*.)

So I smiled and he said, "Watch the court, for God's sake, they've started," and they had.

"That's a point to Collier," he said, and I marked it down and dared not take my eyes off court after that, even to thank him. I looked down again when they changed ends and Carson had gone. (I asked him later where he had gone to and he said he went to throw up. I hope all this doesn't make Carson sound too *coarse*. He was in great pain. It turned out that he had broken a bone in his foot but we didn't know that, then. There are a lot of bones in the foot although you think of it as being solid – down to the toes, at any rate.)

Collier wasn't having it all his own way hooray hooray. Mills was very good too and the first set went to a tie-break. I still wasn't making any mistakes. But when they came off the court after the tie-break which Collier won, and did Wimbledony things with towels and a bit of swigging and spitting, he kept not looking at me. I mean, you could definitely see him *not* looking at me. Everybody could see him *not* looking at me; remembering what he had said about Friday and what I had said about Friday, as loudly as I could.

I was nearly crying again, and what with that and the state of the official school pencil, the score card began to be in a bit of a mess and I suddenly realized that I was putting Collier's points on the wrong line. And of course, I called out, "Advantage Mills," when it should have been 40–30 to Collier and he yelled at me to look at what I was doing.

You don't argue with the umpire. You certainly don't *yell* at the umpire, but he did. I know I was wrong but he didn't have to yell. I kept thinking about him yelling and about Friday and in the next game I made the same mistake again and he was saying, "That's all I need; a cross-eyed umpire. There's eight hundred people in this school can't we find *one* with twenty-twenty vision?" If Fiery Fred or Orang-Evans had heard he might not have, but he was up by the net and facing away from them. He got worse and worse. Abusive.

Then Mills won the next game without any help from me and I thought, at least he's not having another walk-over, and I remembered what Carson had said. "He doesn't care where he puts his feet." And of course, after that, I couldn't help looking at his feet and Carson was right. He didn't care where he put them. He had this very fantastic service that went up about ten yards before he hit the ball, but his toes were over the base line three times out of five. I don't know why nobody noticed. I suppose they were all watching the fantastic ten-yard service and anyway, nobody looks at feet.

At first I forgot that this was anything to do with me; when I did remember I couldn't bear to do anything about it, at first. Then it was Mills who was serving and I had time to think.

I thought, why should he get away with it?

Then I thought, he gets away with everything, and I realized that Carson probably hadn't been talking about real feet but feet was all I could think of.

Collier served. His feet were not where they should have been.

"Fifteen–love."

I thought, I'll give you one more chance, because he was playing so well and I didn't want to spoil that fantastic service. But he had his chance, and he did it again. It was a beautiful shot, an ace, right down the centre line, and Mills never got near it.

I said, "Foot fault."

There was a sort of mumbling noise from everyone watching and Collier scowled but he had to play the second service. Mills tipped it back over the net and Collier never got near it.

"Fifteen all."

"Foot fault."

He was going to argue but of course he couldn't because feet is not what he looked at when he was serving.

"Fifteen–thirty." His second service wasn't very good, really.

"Foot fault."

"Fifteen–forty."

And then he did begin to look, and watching his feet he had to stop watching the ball and all sorts of things began to happen to his service.

Mills won that set.

"What the hell are you playing at, Turner?" said Collier, when they came off court and he called me a vindictive little cow while he was towelling and spitting but honestly, I never called foot fault if it wasn't one.

They went back for the third set and it was Collier's service. He glared at me like he had death-ray eyeballs and tossed up the first ball. And looked up.

And looked down at his feet.

And looked up again, but it was too late and the ball came straight down and bounced and rolled away into the crowd.

So he served again, looked up, looked down, and tried to move back and trod on his own foot and fell over.

People laughed. A laugh sounds terrible on Centre Court with all those walls to bounce off. Some of the algae had transferred itself to his shorts.

By now, *everybody* was looking at his feet.

He served a double fault.

"So who's winning?" said Alan Carson, back again and now looking greener than Collier's shorts. I knew he would understand because he *had* come back instead of going home to pass out which was what he should have been doing.

"I am," I said, miserably.

"Two Pyrrhic victories in one afternoon?" said Alan. "That must be some kind of record."

"It must be," I said. "It's got a hole in it."

SLAM!

WALTER DEAN MYERS

Seventeen-year-old Greg "Slam" Harris is a top man on the basketball court: he plays guard and he plays it good. But his singlemindedness and refusal to compromise bring him into conflict with his coach at Latimer School and with some of the other members of the team.

"OK, LET'S SET THE BIG PICTURE." Mr Nipper had his foot up on a chair. He was wearing a suit and tie with sneakers. He looked OK. "Because of the budget problems in some of the schools we're going to have a short regular season this year and then go to the championship rounds. Maybe next year we can get back to the regular schedule. The way they're trying to make it fair is to make more divisions. There are eight teams in our division and I think we have a chance of doing well. Goldy, you have the list of schools?"

"Regis, St Peter's, Trinity, Country Day, Hunter, Harlem School of the Arts, Carver, and us," Mr Goldstein read off the list.

"Carver handled us pretty easily last year," Mr Nipper said. "But they're in the league and we have to deal with them and everybody else. We'll play each team one time. At the end of the round-robin tournament the two teams with the best records will play each other for the division championship. The division champions will then play for the City PSAL championships.

I'm going to try to schedule a couple of non-league games in, too. Just for the experience.

"So every game is going to be important. If we beat the best teams and lose to the worst we'll still be hurting our record. We have a pretty good squad and we can be there at the end if we play together as a team. We're down to ten players and I'm going to stick with the ten unless somebody gets hurt. That way everybody gets to play. Jimmy's going to be our starting centre. Frank and Tony will be at the forwards and Nick and Trip will be the starting guards, but everybody will get a chance to play."

I was ticked off because I wasn't starting but I figured that once I got to play in a game things would turn around.

Our first game was at home against Regis and when we got out on to the floor they were already warming up. They had some size on us but it didn't look that bad. We ran our warm-up drills and then sat down to wait for the tip-off.

The Regis cheerleaders were looking like they just fell out from a magazine they looked so good. They had the same colour outfits as the ballplayers and they all wore these big red-frame glasses with no glass in them.

Our cheerleaders had a few nice cheers but they weren't as sharp as the ones from Regis. Plus, the people who came to see Regis play had a big banner in the stands. They were looking good.

I thought I heard my name and looked up and saw about five guys from the hood, including Ice. He made a fist and held it up in the air and I held mine up. That just made me feel worse about not starting.

"I want everybody on the bench to stay alert and be ready to go in," Goldy said.

The game started and Regis got the opening tap. The guy that got the tap dribbled right past our whole team and made a layup. That happens sometimes when you first start a game so I didn't think nothing of it.

Trip brought the ball in to Nick and the Panthers had their first offensive play. Nick made a signal and everybody forgot everything they had been doing in practice. Guys were running all over the place and Nick was out there near the top of the key looking for somebody to get open. Finally, he passes the ball in to Jimmy and Jimmy turns and starts a little hook. The centre from Regis went up and slapped Jimmy's shot away and the Regis fans were cheering.

Regis got the ball and came downcourt fast. They passed the ball to one of their forwards coming along the baseline and he passed it to their centre. The centre went up, made the deuce, and got the foul. Jimmy held his hand up because he had fouled the guy.

Their centre made the foul shot and we were behind by five.

Regis was playing a zone but it didn't look that tough because they were just standing around. They kept their hands up but nobody on our team was really challenging their zone. That let them collapse under the basket and box out of the rebounds. We were getting one shot at a time and they weren't even the best shots. The coach put in Glen for Tony Fornay and he moved a little more than Tony did but not enough to change the game.

At the end of the first quarter the score was Regis 18 and Latimer 9. By the half the score was Regis 30 and Latimer 21.

The way it looked was like either school could win. Regis wasn't that good, but the only players on our team who were doing anything was Nick and Trip. Jimmy was standing around the paint so much he got called for two three-second violations, and our forwards looked like they were just throwing the ball towards the backboards and hoping for the best. I looked up at Ice and he just shook his head.

The coach gave a big speech about how we were still in the game and how he wanted every loose ball. We went back out to warm up for the second half and Ice came over to the side of the court and called me over.

"How come you ain't playing?" he asked.

"The coach don't like me or something," I said.

"Tell him I said you need to get some game," Ice said.

I know I needed to get some game. I had been looking forward to playing all day and now I was just sitting on the bench.

"Hey, Greg! Come here!" the coach called me over.

"What's that guy's name?" the coach asked me. "The guy you were talking to just now."

"Benny Reese," I said, using his real name.

"They call him Ice?"

"Yeah."

"That's who I thought it was," he said. Then he walked away.

Hey, that blew my mind. My coach had heard about Ice. Probably had even seen him before.

The first five minutes of the second half was real sloppy. We stunk and so did Regis but they got up by twelve points. Then, when one of their players got fouled, the coach took out both Glen and Frank, moved Jimmy over to forward, put Jose at centre and put Trip at the other forward.

"Greg, get in."

At first I didn't even realize he was talking to me but then Ducky pushed my arm and I woke up. I went over to the scorer's table and reported in.

When I got on the court my homeys started whooping. It made me feel good.

"Yo! Slam! Slam! Slam!" That was from my man Ice.

There hadn't been one dunk in the whole game but I knew there was going to be one soon. I inbounded the ball to Nick and he went down the centre, threw a little head fake on his man, and ran him into a pick. He looked like he was in the clear but when he went up to take his shot their centre, who was knocking everything down, pinned his stuff against the boards and then pulled it down.

On the way downcourt Nick gives me this funny look like he was embarrassed that the Regis centre had thrown away his stuff.

"I'm going for the pill," I said. "Get him if he spins."

Their guard came down centre court and I went after him when he got a foot from the mid-court line. He got over the line all right and spun just the way I thought he might. But Nick came up on his blind side when he saw the spin and knocked the ball away. Nick started downcourt and their whole team was after him.

I was busting tail downcourt when I saw Nick stop and hold up the play. Trip came out to him and got the ball for a hot minute and passed it right back to Nick. But both their forwards were outside with the guards and I got loose on the left side. Nick took a step to the right and threw a hard pass to me. I turned and saw their centre moving towards me.

I put the ball on the floor for a quick beat and then took it to the metal. The pill was cupped between my fingers and my wrist, and I felt the move. It was like the whole thing was going down in slow motion and I was in it and watching it at the same time. Their centre was going up, arching his back away from me so he wouldn't get a body foul, and getting his hands up as high as he could.

I saw his forehead and then I saw the rim and then I felt the pebble grain against my fingertips as I slammed the ball with everything I had. When my palm slapped against the rim it felt good. It felt good.

It was like we had just been out there toying with them before I slammed over their big man. Everybody got into the defence and we started doing some serious ball-hawking. Regis had two guys who could handle the ball pretty good and we had three guys, me, Trip, and Nick, who could go get it. We stole the ball twice and got them in a backcourt violation once. The result was six more points for us and their coach was calling a time-out. We were only down by four.

"See who they're bringing in." The coach pushed Goldy towards the scorer's table.

"How many fouls do I have?" Trip asked. He poured some water on one of the towels and put it on the back of his neck. You could see the excitement on the bench.

"Only two, you're cool."

"We didn't want to give them foul shots," the coach said. "We have to make them work for everything they get."

"They're putting in one of their seniors." Goldy came back to the bench. "He's got to be a ballhandler."

"OK, listen up, guys." The coach knelt down in front of us.

"They're probably going to try to slow the game down and draw fouls. We've got nine minutes to play, that's plenty of time. What we need is board control. We can't let them get second and third shots. Let's go get them!"

We got back on the floor and they inbounded. The coach was right, the new Regis player could handle the ball and they were slowing things down, working the ball in and out, looking for the easy deuce.

My man wasn't doing squat, just running in circles like he was waiting for some dynamite pass, but I think he just didn't want the ball. I started playing him real loose and kept switching off on number 5, Trip's man. He saw me coming and got the pass off to my man at the top of the key, and I turned and ran back to my man. He tried to get rid of the ball back to number 5, but Trip picked it off.

We got downcourt with Trip on the point and Nick cutting across the lane. They picked up Trip and he bounced the ball into me and I was one-on-one with their centre again and I was deep. A fake got him up in the air and I was around him and laid it up for two.

From there on in it was like a practice session. We kept double-teaming the ball and they kept throwing it away. They had lost their nerve. We went up by six, and then by nine with a minute to go.

I wanted one more slam and I got it when Nick and Tony, who was back in the game in Jimmy's place, double-teamed one of their forwards. I could see he was spooked.

"Ball! Ball!" I called to him and he just let it go to me.

The guy who had lost the ball to me was the only one coming after me as I went downcourt. He was two steps behind when I hit the foul line, and when I took my takeoff step he was still on the wood. I went up turning and flying and threw it down on a bad reverse slam and I could hear everybody screaming.

They were still screaming as Regis went through the motions of walking the ball down and watching the clock tick the time off. Twenty seconds . . . ten seconds . . . five . . . and the buzzer went off. We had won by eleven points.

ALEX

TESSA DUDER

In 1958, aged 17, Tessa Duder competed for New Zealand in the international Empire Games, winning a silver medal in the 100 yards butterfly event. She later used this experience in her four books about young champion swimmer Alex Archer. This extract is taken from the first book, Alex, which tells of the teenager's efforts to beat her arch rival Maggie Benton and qualify for the 1960 Rome Olympics. It all hinges on the result of the sprint final – just two lengths of the pool. Alex is desperate to win, not only for herself but for Andy, her boyfriend, who has recently died. I have reproduced this account of Alex's thoughts as she swims the race as a continuous narrative, though in the book it is split into parts that begin each chapter. To me, this piece stands well on its own; it really gets you under a racing swimmer's skin.

I HAVE ALWAYS KNOWN that in another life I was – or will be – a dolphin. I'm silver and grey, the sleekest thing on fins, with a permanent smile on my face. I leap over and through the waves. I choose a passing yacht to dive under and hear the shouts of the children as I emerge triumphant close to the boat.

Right at this moment, I'd give anything for that freedom. I am a pink human, caught in a net of ambition and years of hard work. In a few minutes I will dive into that artificially turquoise water waiting at my feet. A minute later I'll be either ecstatic or a failure.

I stare at my toes, which are white with fright. How will I ever get my legs going with feet of marble? I step from one foot to the other. My arms describe drunken windmills. I'll need all the oxygen I can get: I breathe in long slow lungfuls. My heart is already pumping away as if it has gone berserk.

I hear "In Lane three, Alexandra Archer" and something else, which is lost in cheers. Automatically I step on to the starting-block. "In Lane four, Maggie Benton," in the lane I wanted to be in, should have been in. Cheers and shouts for her, too. More than for me, or less? I have never been able to tell. What does it matter, anyway? I stand head down. Nothing will make me look at her. Since we hugged goodbye this morning we have avoided each other, carefully not being in the dressing room at the same time, not meeting in doorways, sitting well apart in the competitors' enclosure. I hope she is feeling as ghastly as me.

We all step down. I walk back to the chair where a woman in a blazer waits to take my track suit. My hands are shaking so much that I can't get my fingers latched on to the tab of the zip. She helps me. Yes, I did put my swimsuit on under all this, my most special pair. People haven't, in the past, from nerves.

Then comes the gold chain, bearing my most precious possession in all the world, Andy's pearl, his tear. It goes deep into my track suit pocket, along with his parents' telegram.

I'm cold, so cold . . . appalled at what I have to do. I stand tall, centre stage, on the first rung of the starting-block. Under the night sky, I feel almost naked. Just me, the body Alex, fit, ready, dangerous.

A whistle blows somewhere. I climb up to the block, as to a guillotine. Shouts and cheers echo around the packed stands. "Maggie", "Alex", "Come on, Maggie", "Go Alex". Then, silence falls like a curtain.

I make a last adjustment to the cap clinging to my ears, a last swing of the arms, shake of the feet, shrug of the shoulders. I hear the breakers of my nightmares crash on the nearby beach. I need a pee.

"Take your marks."

I curl my toes carefully around the edge of the block. It's a

169

relief to bend my knees. I crouch down, hearing the wrench of cartilage in knee joints, and look along the fifty-five yards of smooth blue water in front of me. Up and back we'll go, flat out. I feel tired already.

Heads or tails? This throw is for you, Andy.

Beside me someone starts to move.

Bang!

Alex, you're dead.

Maggie's got a flyer on you. A glorious flyer.

You're beaten before you even start.

My fingertips slice open the water. Briefly I'm an arrow, piercing the blue with every muscle taut, making the most of the thrust from the block.

I dare not trust my mid-flight ears. I think I heard the whistle for a false start. From bitter experience I know I cannot assume anything.

Legs begin to kick. The first strokes, and then with both relief and disgust I'm pulled up short by the rope. It's like a physical blow, rasping roughly across my arms and sending shock waves juddering down to my feet.

Damn and blast! False starts break the spell, break confidence, break rhythm, everything! One often leads to two, and then we're all in dead trouble.

We swim slowly back, trying to get shattered nerves together. Blast and damn you, Maggie; but at least that's one race you're not going to win with a flyer. In the water, a fair fight.

"If there's a break, go with it. Don't waste energy on getting angry." Mr Jack's last words, among others. "Use the time in the water to relax. Get out last. Keep them waiting those few seconds. Maggie will be just as thrown off balance." So she will; so she is. Maggie hasn't done a false start in years. She's rattled.

I look at no one as I haul myself out last, shaking the water off my arms. The starter, immaculate in white, is already waiting to give his pep talk. Already I can feel the coldness seeping through my feet. A sweet man, but get on with it. We line up the second time.

"Take your marks." We bend down, and then someone does it again.

Maggie stays poised on the brink, so do I. The rest have gone in. Tears of frustration blur my vision. And fear: break on the third time and you're out, Alex, finish, kaput. A humiliating way to let you down, Andy.

The crowd has nearly gone wild. Again the pep talk, though this time we are allowed to get towels and track suit tops for a laughable attempt at staying warm. "Take it easy, girls. Next one who breaks is out. I'll hold you till every last one is rock steady. There'll be no flyers here." I look over to where Mr Jack and Dad are sitting, but there is only a blur of faces, eyes, spotlights. This is the event of these nationals, my long-awaited clash with Maggie, the fight to the death. A capacity house, fanfares, overture and beginners please. Reporters' pens dipped in blood. I badly need a pee.

Toes around the block. A dreadful hush. I am cold through and through, literally trembling at the knees, devoid of any thought. I only know that I must not allow myself to break; neither must I be so cautious I get left behind at the starting post and throw that vital fraction of a second and the race away.

"Take your marks!"

An intolerable silence. There's not a movement. About five hours pass. My ears are out on stalks.

Bang.

We hit the water as one. This time I notice that the water feels warm, a sure sign of creeping coldness.

We're off to see the Wizard . . .

Warm, water, glaring underwater lights, and the black shark that is Maggie right alongside me. Surprisingly, my arms feel good, rhythm feels good, at one with the water. It's not always so, especially after false starts; five seconds into a race your chest can be tight, arms sluggish and legs like lead. Then it's hard going all the way, fighting the water, fighting pain and anger.

Anger. Now there's an interesting sort of fuel. After the events of today, I'm fairly loaded with it, and taking off like a rocket. Ten yards down and still I've not taken a breath.

We're spread out in a line across the pool. Soon, about a third of the way down, one head will be seen by the crowd to be marginally in front, the point of the arrow. It must be me. But beware, not only Maggie, but the complete outsider who could beat us both to the turn and then hang on like grim death. Unlikely, but not impossible. In sprints, settled in hundredths of a second, stranger things have happened.

People ask me what I think about when I'm swimming. Right now I hate everyone. I hate Maggie and what she might yet snatch from my grasp, and even more I hate adults who jump to conclusions and spread untrue gossip.

First round is to me. On this lap, where the water is smooth, I can see Maggie's white bathing cap cruising along when I take my first breaths. Hey, Andy . . . I'm about a hand's breadth in front.

There's a long way to go yet, Alex.

Concentrate!

One hand has brushed the corks that make up the lane ropes. That might cost me a hundredth of a second, and the race. Can't you swim straight, even now, just once, Alex, your last chance?

Concentrate! The turn is coming up. It must be nothing less than perfect. Races and trips have been decided on a single turn.

Into deeper water, darker blue glass. On both sides, through the criss-cross patterns of underwater lights, are bodies hard at work. I'm leading.

And not only by a hand, more an arm's length. What has happened? "Go out hard," Mr Jack said. (I've done that.) "Pile on the pressure." (That too.) "You'll need every bit you can get for the return journey, flying blind."

The turn, idiot! Where are the red lane markers, the black lines on the bottom of the pool, to judge how far? I have a moment of sheer panic that I've missed them and am about to slam into the wall. I'm nine years old again.

I got all three turns right in the two hundred and twenty yards two days ago. It was one of those races where everything clicked. That, and pushing myself past the pain barrier into a silence where I swear I heard Andy call my name, was why, contrary to all expectations, I won it! The quarter-mile on Tuesday had been Maggie's. I had to win the two hundred and twenty to stay in the running. One each, then, and Mrs Benton up to all sorts of mischief. Why can't you just leave Maggie and me alone to slog it out?

This is the decider, here and now, for Rome. May the best woman win, and her mother go to hell.

Despite the false starts, I'm feeling good. I'm flying over the water with that delight in my own speed, my own power, which only comes when everything is right. Make the most of it. The pain, the real work is yet to come.

Five yards to the turn. Right or left arm will touch? Alarm bells ring. Prepare to dive!

Help me, Andy!

Looking ahead through my bow wave, I see the glint of blue tile.

In the end it's instinct that determines which hand will touch, plus a few years' experience! Maggie's flip I know to be neater, with her shorter legs, and more reliable; mine is less dependable, but when it really works, fantastic.

It's that sort I need. Right now. The right hand touches, slides down the wall. Follow it down, legs shoot over. If it's a good one, feet will be close to the wall for a good strong push-off.

I'm over! I've seen a flash of black in the lane next door. My legs thrust backwards, hopefully sending me off towards the finish like a catapult. I'm Archer and Arrow again, taut from fingertip to toe-tip.

But you've slipped, Alex! Your toes have not gripped the wall. Your push-off makes the best of a bad job, but is feeble compared with what it could have been. An eighty per cent push. Your leg reminds you that a few months ago it had problems of its own. You know without looking that the black torpedo in the next lane has done one of its neat, reliable turns and thrust itself into the lead.

Damn you, Maggie. And damn you even more, Alex's feet, for costing you the trip to Rome. Six year's work, sliding sideways off a patch of tile.

All you watching and yelling people, cheer for me no longer.

Alex has blown it. I can just hear the radio announcer . . . "They've turned, Miss Archer just slightly ahead, a magnificent first lap, under thirty seconds, there could be a record here, no it's Miss Benton who comes out in front, what a magnificent turn, half a yard ahead now as they begin to stroke . . ."

Alex has blown it. She is screaming and crying too, with anger and shame. You fool!

The first stroke, a breath because my lungs are bursting and there's worse to come, and even though Maggie is now on my blind side I can see enough out of the corner of my right eye to know that she has a full yard on me.

I'm sorry, Andy. My gift – resolutions, intentions, determinations – was not enough.

"If you're ahead after the turn, don't let up. If you're not, my only advice is put your head down and gofurrit."

I am now goingfurrit, Mr Jack, truly I am. Breathing every second stroke, because I've used up nearly all my puff on the first lap and the going's getting rough.

This part of the race I loathe. The tops of your arms are aching, and every breath is your last gasp and you've yet to go into the overdrive where you forget you're dying and the only thing that's left in the world is getting to that solid wall at the end.

There's always the stupid hope that Maggie will somehow slow down, take a mouthful, hit a lane-rope, get a stomach cramp – anything. But she never does. She swims like a true pro. As Andy says, "That's why she keeps winning, because swimming is her life."

Hasn't it been my life? So much so that I've been obsessed by it, even to the point of not noticing Gran was fading away to a shadow, and Julia had just a wee problem with that Australian uncle of hers.

I'm not going to make it. It's all been too much, really.

I'm retiring as of now. Good luck for Rome, Maggie. I'll find someone who's got a television and watch you on that.

Don't give in, Alex. Never give in. Forty yards to go yet.

Andy, have pity.

I can't keep this up.

If you really mean business, you have to keep it up, Alex, and more.

Am I gaining on her, Andy? Pinned her back a hand's breadth, a finger, a fingernail even?

This is for real, maybe the first race in my life at total one hundred per cent effort, where desperation and rage have added their fuel to ambition, and afterwards I will be able to look Mr Jack and Dad and Mum and Gran and the kids and Miss Gillies and Maggie and even Mrs Benton in the face and say I could not have tried harder.

Breathing is uphill and every arm stroke a circle of pain. My legs, shaved so carefully in the shower tonight, are tingling, almost as though being massaged by the water. It's a feeling I've not had often; a signal that my body is about to go into another gear.

I think I'm gaining. I can no longer see much. I dare not upset my rhythm and take a breath to the right. I never learnt to breathe right-handed. It always felt as awkward as breathing to the left was natural. The water is choppy and I can't tell whether the arms and legs flailing away next door are ahead or even with me. But I think I'm gaining.

Andy, tell me, I need to know. Am I? Am I?

I am! I can, Andy! I'm closing the gap.

Breathing each stroke now, because I've no breath left for anything else.

Too late? Thrown away at the turn, with that feeble push-off?

But I'm feeling good, strong. I'm riding up over my bow wave. One race in five, perhaps, comes this surge, this incredible sensation that I'm being pulled, propelled through the water by some invisible force, not just my own muscles.

I'm in overdrive, relentless. Pain has gone. I know I can do it now. I'm almost flying.

Coming to get you, Maggie Benton. This'll teach you, Maggie Benton, bringing coaches in from Australia for special coaching all to yourself and not telling anyone. Only that you'd gone out of town to train for the week before the nationals. It took a few days for the grapevine to shake out the news that the coach you'd had in Queensland last August holidays just happened to be in the same place the same week. Funny that.

I hate to spoil your little plans, Mrs Benton, but Aussie coaches or not, Maggie's not going to win this race. You can spend all the money you like, but when we get in the pool we're all equal.

You can't blame your equipment like most other sports, or the weather, or being put off by someone screaming instructions from the sideline. There's just your body and a whole lot of water to get through faster than any other body. Your body, and your will, against hers.

You're not level yet, Alex. She's holding you off. She's not beaten yet. Oh, what's twenty seconds of agony after what you've been through in the last eight months? Don't chuck it away . . .

Andy, I hear you. But I'm hurting like hell . . .

Some things I do know, Andy. Round about here, races are won or lost. Maggie, for the first time in her life, too, is swimming this race to win. Never mind what the stop-watch says. And she's increased her stroking rate.

I've gained, yet still she holds me off. Half a yard, a hand? Are my arms that much longer when it comes to the final lunge for the wall?

No, they're not. I've mighty long arms, like an albatross, a wing span of over two yards, but that's not long enough.

Round about here races are lost, Alex. Oh think ahead, sweet maid, to the wall, to Rome.

That Aussie coach sitting out there with Lady Benton. He might ask me to join his squad in Queensland . . . what about a scholarship to an American university . . .

Put that in your pipe, Mrs Benton. Oh I'm slipping, I'm slipping, I'm going backwards for Christmas . . .

Alex, you're not concentrating. Your stroke rate – can you move up a notch?

Did you say stroke faster, Andy? I'll try, oh I'll try, though my lungs are bursting.

Through the splash, through bathing cap tight against ears, I can hear the roar of the crowd. It must be loud.

They don't care who wins, not really. It's just a good race to them, another good battle, like gladiators in the Roman arena slogging it out. One dies, one will live, they don't care which.

But Mr Jack cares, and my family cares like hell, even Jamie in his own funny way, and Andy does, would have, does.

You care, Alex . . . more than anyone, you care, says Andy. So get cracking.

How much does she still have, Andy? Between me and Rome, me and oblivion – between Maggie the winner and me the loser . . .

She still has something, Alex. You'll have to try harder.

I can't.

I think you can.

It's not fair, for a trip to hang on the result of one race!

Consider yourself luckier than the Americans. They have trials for their Olympic teams. It doesn't matter if you hold a world record, if you get beaten in the trials, that's it. One trial, one race, one chance.

Perhaps they might send both of us?

It's possible. Your times are good enough.

Even if she wins this, I hold the national record.

You're on your way to another.

You're kidding.

Honest. First lap was under thirty seconds. Turn wasn't too hot, you lost about point four there . . .

And lost the race.

Oh no. She's only got about six inches on you now.

That's all? No kidding?

That's all. Dig in, girl . . .

I've been thinking what you said about both of us going to Rome, Andy. I read something this week, that swimming commentator in the *Weekly News*, some old boy who's been doing it for years. Anyway, predictions:

"Whatever the outcome of the national titles, serious consideration should be given to sending both these talented girls to Rome. Their intense rivalry over five seasons has already inspired a new generation of juniors and can only go on benefitting the sport.

"Miss Benton has the more impressive score of titles and records over the season, and has proved herself a consistent and graceful champion. But time and time again she has been pushed to these achievements by the brave and determined Miss Archer, whose potential is, if anything, the greater. One must win the lion's share in Napier, but both should be considered worthy for Rome . . ." Isn't that great?

Alex, you're d-dodging the issue, already looking for boltholes . . .

I am not . . .

Yes you are. Don't you realize you're absolutely neck-and-neck. Twenty yards to go and you're already justifying second place . . . hoping it will be good enough for Rome.

All right then I am. I simply cannot go any faster. And I've got my period, a week early. My body is telling me something.

So? It has never worried you in the past. You've won races with your period before.

You know me too well.

Wasn't this win for me?

Perhaps I just haven't got what it takes, not really. I should've listened to you that day when I jumped off your boat, saved myself a whole lot of work. You were right.

I was wrong. But you've got to do it. No one can win for you. Oh, keep trying, sweet maid . . . Hold on . . .

What a fool! I've just remembered, Andy. The race nearly gone and I've only just flicked up, she can't see me either. We're both flying blind!

That's right, you chump. Don't think you're the only one with the handicaps. Maggie's frightened out of her tiny mind.

She's never. This time she is. She knows you've got longer arms than her. You can lunge for the wall.

I should take up fencing.

You could try winning this race first. Ten yards. The crowd is going wild.

I can see them when I turn my head, people on the side of the pool, arms waving . . .

Don't worry about them. Say after me . . . First, Alexandra Archer . . .

First, Alexandra Archer . . . I'm dying, Andy. My arms are falling off . . . I stopped breathing about a minute ago.

First, Alexandra Archer. Second, Alexandra Archer.

Ninety-fifth, Alexandra Archer . . . Also ran, Alexandra Archer . . . Go, Alex, Alex, go . . .

You can hear the crowd, Alex? It's pandemonium down there, Alex. Your father's on his feet, Gran's actually standing on the bench, jumping up and down, Mr Jack is still sitting on his butt biting the quicks of his nails. He can't bear to look.

I bet Mrs Benton can't either.

She's gone very pale. The Aussie coach beside her has just said something about that Archer girl's got courage, great fighter, and she's just bit his head off. He's come right back at her and says he knows real talent and spirit when he sees it, and Mrs Benton thinks he's getting at Maggie, putting her down, and no one's ever done that, ever, and for once in her life she's speechless.

Serve the woman right. Though not fair to Maggie.

Maggie's scared out of her brain. Not really losing to you. She's got a lot of time for you . . .

It's mutual.

Her mother's face. Disapproval, disappointment, written all

over. That's what Maggie's afraid of, guilt, letting her mother down. It's going to take her another whole year to come to terms with it, not until . . . No, I mustn't say that, not yet.

I've beaten her before . . .

This time is special. It has become more than just a swimming race to you. Why else are you pushing yourself past your limit . . .

True. Oh Andy, when will it end . . .

You're doing well. Courage . . .

Five yards Alex. Maggie's as desperate as you are. Her stroke has disintegrated a bit. Her mother is frozen, still as a stone, white-faced. She thinks it's all over.

My stroke went out the window ages ago. I feel like some sort of crazy windmill.

Looks good to me. I've always loved watching you swim, Alex, the sheer power of you. I get the same feeling watching dolphins in the sea out from the beach.

I was thinking of dolphins earlier.

Wait till afterwards, concentrate on what you're doing. Three yards, Alex, she thinks she's got you . . .

Andy, help me, please . . . I want, so badly . . . to win.

Two yards, Alex. There's nothing in it, nothing. You just need a fingernail that's all. Oh, Alex, stretch, reach . . .

God's teeth, Andy . . .

For me . . .

I'm dead, Andy. I have nothing left.

You have, a fingernail, that's all you need . . .

I haven't even got that. I bit them all off years ago. You know how awful my nails are . . .

For God's sake, shut up. You are so near a record, over a second off.

You're kidding me again.

Listen, woman, would I lie?

I've shot my bolt . . .

Don't be crude. Just throw yourself at the wall . . .

What do you think I'm doing?

Reach for a star, Alex. The one I'm holding out . . . The gold one with a record and Rome written on it . . .

I'm nine years old and it's my first race again and I'm swimming so fast that I try to swim right through the end of the pool.

Two strokes, one. I'm swimming up a waterfall. I'm at the bottom of the sea. I've drowned.

I've touched, with an arm I swear grew five inches. Later I'll find all my fingers are bruised.

All movement stops. It has stopped in the next lane too, where Maggie lies on her back gasping like a fish in extremis. I can hear nothing, see nothing. I hang over the lane ropes. I will never swim another race as long as I live. I don't think I'll survive to tell the tale.

Gradually, I'm aware of a crowd on its feet, applause, cheering; thankfully, because my body is making most peculiar noises as I draw in great lungfuls of air. I am strangely uninterested in the result.

Liar, he says. Anyway, you know, don't you?

Do I? Dare I?

Yes, you'll dare anything now.

It was supposed to be my gift to you.

It was. You gave me yourself, the greatest gift of all. Now stand up. You're the champ. Enjoy the rituals. Maggie wants to congratulate you. You can enjoy being friends now. You're both going to Rome, you know, but don't tell her just yet.

You knew? All the time?

Of course.

Through all that? Killing myself . . . You knew?

My gift was hope. *Arrivederci*. I loved you, sweet maid . . .

Andy?

Arrivederci . . .

Before you leave me, I love you too . . .

THE RUNNING-COMPANION

PHILIPPA PEARCE

ANY DAY, over the great expanses of the Common, you can see runners. In track-suits or shorts and running-tops, they trot along the asphalted paths across the grass, or among the trees, or by the Ponds. On the whole, they avoid London Hill, towards the middle of the Common, because of its steepness. There is another reason. People climb the Hill for the magnificence of the view of London from the top; but runners consider it unlucky, especially at dusk. They say it is haunted by ghosts and horrors then. One ghost; one horror.

In his lifetime, Mr Kenneth Adamson was one of the daily runners. This was a good many years ago now. His story has been pieced together from what was reported in the newspapers, what was remembered by neighbours and eye-witnesses, and what may have been supposed to have been going on in the mind of Mr Adamson himself.

Sometimes Mr Adamson ran on the Common in the early morning; more often he ran in the evening after work. He worked in an office. He was not liked there: he was silent, secretive, severe. People were afraid of him.

The Adamsons lived in one of the terrace-houses bordering the Common. There was old Mrs Adamson, a widow, who hardly comes into this story at all; and her two sons, of whom Kenneth, or Ken, was the elder. There were only two people in the world who called Mr Adamson by his first name: they were his mother and his brother. He had no wife or girlfriend; no friends at all.

Mr Adamson ran daily in order to keep himself fit. The steady jog-trot of this kind of running soothed his whole being; even his mind was soothed. While his legs ran a familiar track, his mind ran along an equally familiar one. Ran, and then ran back, and then ran on again: his mind covered the same ground over and over and over again.

His mind ran on hatred.

Mr Adamson's hatred was so well grown and in such constant training that at times it seemed to him like another living being. In his mind there were the three of them: himself; and his hatred; and his brother, the object of his hatred.

Of course, Mr Adamson's brother never ran. He could not walk properly without a crutch; he could only just manage to get upstairs and downstairs by himself in their own house. He had been crippled in early childhood, in an accident; and his mother had not only cared for him, but spoilt him. To Mr Adamson's way of thinking, she had neglected *him*. Jealousy had been the beginning of Mr Adamson's hatred, in childhood: as the jealousy grew, the hatred grew, like a poison tree in his mind. It grew all the more strongly because Mr Adamson had always kept quiet about it: he kept his hatred quiet inside his mind.

He grew up; and his hatred grew with him.

For years now Mr Adamson's hatred had been with him, not only when he ran, but all day, and often at night, too. Sometimes in his dreams it seemed to him that his running-companion, his hatred, stood just behind him, or at his very elbow, a person. By turning his head he would be able to see that person. He knew that his hatred was full-grown now; and he longed to know what it looked like. Was it monster or man? Had it a heavy body, like his own, to labour uphill only with effort; or had it a real runner's physique, lean and leggy? He had only to turn his head and see; but in his dreams he was always prevented.

184

"Ken!"

His mother's thin old voice, calling his name up the stairs, would break into his dreams, summoning him down to breakfast. Mr Adamson breakfasted alone, listening to the sound of his brother moving about in his room above, or perhaps beginning his slow, careful descent of the stairs. Listening to that, it seemed to Mr Adamson that he heard something else: a friend's voice at his ear, whispering a promise: "One day, Ken . . ."

One day, at last, Mrs Adamson died of old age. The two brothers were left alone together in the house on the edge of the Common. They would have to manage, people said. On the morning after the funeral, Mr Adamson prepared the day's meals, then went off to his office. At this time of year, he ran in the evenings, never in the mornings. It was the beginning of autumn and still pleasant on the Common in the evening, in spite of the mist.

Mr Adamson came home from work; and presumably the two brothers had supper, talked perhaps – although Mr Adamson never spoke to his brother if he could help it – and prepared for bed. Just before bedtime, as usual, Mr Adamson must have changed into his running shorts and top and training shoes and set off on his evening run.

Questioned afterwards, the neighbours said that the evening seemed no different from any other evening. But how were they to know? The Adamsons lived in a house whose party-walls let little noise through. Would they have heard a cry of fear: "Ken – no!" Would they have heard a scream? The sound of a heavy body falling – falling –?

Some time that evening Mr Adamson's brother fell downstairs, fatally, from the top of the stairs to the bottom. Whether he fell by his own mischance (but no, in all his life, he had never had an accident on those stairs), or whether he was pushed – nothing was ever officially admitted. But the evidence examined afterwards at least pointed to his already lying there at the foot of the stairs, huddled, still, when Mr Adamson went out for his evening run. Mr Adamson must have had to step over his dead body as he came downstairs, in his running gear, to go out on the Common.

It so happened that neighbours did see Mr Adamson leaving the house. He left it looking as usual – or almost as usual, they said. One neighbour remarked that Mr Adamson seemed to be smiling. He never smiled, normally. They saw no one come out of the house with him, of course. No one followed him.

Mr Adamson set off across the Common, as usual increasing his pace until it reached a jog-trot. This was the speed that suited him. Joints loosened; heartbeats and breathing steadied; the air was on his face; only the sky above him. His mind felt both satisfied and empty: free. This was going to be the run of his life.

He planned to run across the Common to the Ponds; then take the main exit route from the Common, leading to the bus terminus and shopping centre; but he would veer away just before reaching them, taking a side path that circled the base of London Hill; and so home.

When he got home, he would ring the doctor or the police, or both, to report his brother's accident. He had no fear of the police. No fear of anyone.

Now, as he ran, he began to get his second wind, and to feel that he could run forever. No, the police would never catch up with him. No one could ever catch up with him.

Pleasantly he ran as far as the Ponds, whose shores were deserted even of ducks. Mist was rising from the water, as dusk descended from the sky. Mr Adamson wheeled round by the Ponds and took the path towards the terminus and shopping centre. He was running well; it seemed to him, superbly.

A runner going well is seldom aware of the sound of his own footfalls, even on an asphalted surface. But Mr Adamson began to notice an odd, distant echo of his own footsteps: perhaps, he thought, an effect of the mist, or of the nearness of London Hill.

Running, he listened to the echo. Unmistakably, running footsteps in the distance: a most curious effect.

Running, listening carefully, he began to change his mind. Those distant footsteps were neither his own nor an echo of his own, after all. Someone behind him was running in the same direction as himself, trotting so exactly at his own pace that he had been deceived into supposing echoes. The footsteps were not so very far in the distance, either. Although the pace was so exactly his own, yet the footsteps of the other runner seemed all the time to be coming a little nearer. The impossibility of this being so made Mr Adamson want to laugh, for the first time in many years. But you don't laugh as you run.

Very slightly, Mr Adamson increased the pace of his running, and maintained it; and listened. The runner behind seemed also to have very slightly increased his pace: the footsteps were a little more rapid, surely, and clearer. Clearer? *Nearer?* Mr Adamson had intended to leave the main way across the Common only just before it reached the terminus and shops: now he decided to take a side path at once. It occurred to him that the runner might just be someone hurrying to catch a bus from the terminus. That supposition was a relief.

He turned along the side path; and the feet behind, in due time, turned too. They began to follow Mr Adamson along the side path, never losing ground, very slightly gaining it.

Mr Adamson quickened his pace yet again: he was now running faster than he liked. He decided to double back to the main path, across the grass.

The grass was soft and silent under his feet. He heard nothing of his own footfalls; he heard no footfalls behind him. Now he was on the main path again, and he still could hear nothing behind him. Thankfully he prepared to slacken his pace.

Then he heard them. The runner behind him must have crossed the soundless grass at a different angle from his own. The strange runner's feet now struck the asphalt of the path behind Mr Adamson nearer than he could possibly have expected – much nearer.

The pace was still the same as his own, yet gained upon him very slightly all the time. He had no inclination to laugh now. He ran faster – faster. The sweat broke on him, ran into his eyes, almost blinding him.

He reached his intended turning off the main path and took it. The feet, in due time, followed him. Too late he wished that he had continued on the main path right to the bus terminus and the shops, to the bright lights of streets and buses and shops. But now he had turned back over the Common, duskier and mistier than ever. He had before him the long path winding round the base of London Hill before it took him home. It was a long way, and a lonely, unfrequented one at this time of evening. The Hill was straight ahead of him, and he knew there would be groups of people at the top, people who walked there in the evening to admire the view. Never before had he chosen to go where there were other human beings, just because they were other human beings, flesh and blood like himself. Now he did. He took the path that led directly to the summit of the Hill.

The evening strollers on the top of the Hill had been looking at the view, and one or two had begun to watch the runner on the slopes below. He was behaving oddly. They had watched him change course, and then double to and fro – "like a rabbit with something after it", as one watcher said.

"He's coming this way," said another.

"Straight up the Hill," observed someone else in the little crowd. Most of them were now peering down through the dusk. "Straight up the Hill – you need to be young and really in training for that."

Straight up the Hill he went, his heart hammering against his ribs, his breath tearing in and out of his throat, his whole body dripping with sweat. He ran and ran, and behind him came the feet, gaining on him.

On the Hill, they were all staring now at the runner. "What's got into him?" someone asked. "You might think all the devils in hell were after him."

"He'll kill himself with running," said a young woman. But she was wrong.

Now he was labouring heavily up the steepest part of the slope, almost exhausted. He hardly ran; rather, staggered. Behind him the feet kept their own pace; they did not slow, as his had done. They would catch up with him soon.

Very soon now.

He knew from the loudness of the following feet that the other runner was at his back. He had only to turn his head and

he would see him face to face; but that he would not do – that he would never do, to save his very soul.

The footsteps were upon him; a voice close in his ear whispered softly – oh! so softly! – and lovingly – oh! so lovingly! "Ken!" it whispered, and would not be denied.

The watchers on the Hill peered down.

"Why has he stopped?"

"Why's he turning round?"

"What's he – Oh, my God!"

For Mr Adamson had turned, and seen what none of the watchers on the Hill could see, and he gave a shriek that carried far over the Common and lost itself in darkness and distance – a long, long shriek that will never be forgotten by any that heard it.

He fell where he stood, in a twisted heap.

When they reached him, he was dead. Overstrain of the heart, the doctor said later; but, being a wise man, he offered no explanation of the expression on Mr Adamson's face. There was horror there and – yes, something like dreadful recognition.

All this happened a good many years ago now; but runners on the Common still avoid London Hill, because of Mr Adamson and whatever came behind him. There may be some runners who fear on their own account – fear the footsteps that might follow them, fear to turn and see the face of their own dearest, worst wickedness. Let us hope not.

YOU KNOW ME AL

RING LARDNER

One of America's finest short story writers, Ring Lardner, started out as a sports columnist for the Chicago Tribune. You Know Me Al *first appeared in serial form in the* Saturday Evening Post *in 1914. In a series of rambling, badly-spelt and conceited letters to his friend Al, rookie White Sox pitcher Jack Keefe relates his ups and downs in the baseball world. The story is full of jokes – mainly at the teller's expense, as Keefe constantly gets on the wrong side of coach Callahan with his often idiotic remarks. In this extract Keefe makes his debut in major league baseball – with mixed results.*

CLEVELAND, OHIO, APRIL 10.

OLD FRIEND AL: Well Al we are all set to open the season this afternoon. I have just ate breakfast and I am sitting in the lobby of the hotel. I eat at a little lunch counter about a block from here and I saved seventy cents on breakfast. You see Al they give us a dollar a meal and if we don't want to spend that much all right. Our rooms at the hotel are paid for.

The Cleveland papers say Walsh or Scott will work for us this afternoon. I asked Callahan if there was any chance of me getting into the first game and he says I hope not. I don't know what he meant but he may surprise these reporters and let me pitch. I will beat them Al. Lajoie and Jackson is supposed to be great batters but the bigger they are the harder they fall.

191

The second team joined us yesterday in Chi and we practised a little. Poor Allen was left in Chi last night with four others of the recruit pitchers. Looks pretty good for me eh Al? I only seen Gleason for a few minutes on the train last night. He says, Well you ain't took off much weight. You're hog fat. I says Oh I ain't fat. I didn't need to take off no weight. He says One good thing about it if the club don't have to engage no birth for you because you spend all your time in the dining car. We kidded along like that a while and then the trainer rubbed my arm and I went to bed. Well Al I just got time to have my suit pressed before noon.

Yours truly, JACK.

Cleveland, Ohio, April 11.
FRIEND AL: Well Al I suppose you know by this time that I did not pitch and that we got licked. Scott was in there and he didn't have nothing. When they had us beat four to one in the eight inning Callahan told me to go out and warm up and he put a batter in for Scott in our ninth. But Cleveland didn't have to play their ninth so I got no chance to work. But looks like he means to start me in one of the games here. We got three more to play. Maybe I will pitch this afternoon. I got a postcard from Violet. She says Beat them Naps. I will give them a battle Al if I get a chance.

Glad to hear you boys have fixed it up to come to Chi during the Detroit serious. I will ask Callahan when he is going to pitch me and let you know. Thanks Al for the papers.

Your friend, JACK.

St Louis, Missouri, April 15.
FRIEND AL: Well Al I guess I showed them. I only worked one inning but I guess them Browns is glad I wasn't in there no longer than that. They had us beat seven to one in the sixth and Callahan pulls Benz out. I honestly felt sorry for him but he didn't have nothing, not a thing. They was hitting him so hard I thought they would score a hundred runs. A righthander name Bumgardner was pitching for them and he didn't look to have nothing either but we ain't got much of a batting team Al. I could hit better than some of them regulars. Anyway Callahan called

Benz to the bench and sent for me. I was down in the corner warming up with Kuhn. I wasn't warmed up good but you know I got the nerve Al and I run right out there like I meant business. There was a man on second and nobody out when I come in. I didn't know who was up there but I found out afterward it was Shotten. He's the centrefielder. I was cold and I walked him. Then I got warmed up good and I made Johnston look like a boob. I give him three fast balls and he let two of them go by and missed the other one. I would of handed him a spitter but Schalk kept signing for fast ones and he knows more about them batters than me. Anyway I whiffed Johnston. Then up come Williams and I tried to make him hit at a couple of bad ones. I was in the hole with two balls and nothing and come right across the heart with my fast one. I wish you could of saw the hop on it. Williams hit it right straight up and Lord was camped under it. Then up come Pratt the best hitter on their club. You know what I done to him don't you Al? I give him one spitter and another he didn't strike at that was a ball. Then I come back with two fast ones and Mister Pratt was a dead baby. And you notice they didn't steal no bases neither.

In our half of the seventh inning Weaver and Schalk got on and I was going up there with a stick when Callahan calls me back and sends Easterly up. I don't know what kind of managing you call that. I hit good on the training trip and he must of knew they had no chance to score off me in the innings they had left while they were liable to murder his other pitchers. I come back to the bench pretty hot and I says You're making a mistake. He says If Comiskey had wanted you to manage this team he would of hired you.

Then Easterly pops out and I says Now I guess you're sorry you didn't let me hit. That sent him right up in the air and he bawled me awful. Honest Al I would of cracked him right in the jaw if we hadn't been right out where everybody could of saw us. Well he sent Cicotte in to finish and they didn't score no more and we didn't either.

I road down in the car with Gleason. He says Boy you shouldn't ought to talk like that to Cal. Some day he will lose his temper and bust you one. I says He won't never bust me. I says He didn't have no right to talk like that to me. Gleason says I suppose you think he's going to laugh and smile when we lost four out of the first five games. He says Wait till to-night and then go up to him and let him know you are sorry you sassed him. I says I didn't sass him and I ain't sorry.

So after supper I seen Callahan sitting in the lobby and I went over and sit down by him. I says When are you going to let me work? He says I wouldn't never let you work only my pitchers are all shot to pieces. Then I told him about you boys coming up from Bedford to watch me during the Detroit serious and he says Well I will start you in the second game against Detroit. He says But I wouldn't if I had any pitchers. He says A girl could get out there and pitch better than some of them have been doing.

So you see Al I am going to pitch on the nineteenth. I hope you guys can be up there and I will show you something. I know I can beat them Tigers and I will have to do it even if they are Violet's team.

I notice that New York and Boston got trimmed to-day so I suppose they wish Comiskey would ask for waivers on me. No chance Al.

Your old pal, JACK.

P.S.—We play eleven games in Chi and then go to Detroit. So I will see the little girl on the twenty-ninth.

Oh you Violet.

Chicago, Illinois, April 19.
DEAR OLD PAL: Well Al it's just as well you couldn't come. They beat me and I am writing you this so as you will know the truth about the game and not get a bum steer from what you read in the papers.

I had a sore arm when I was warming up and Callahan should never ought to of sent me in there. And Schalk kept signing for my fast ball and I kept giving it to him because I thought he ought to know something about the batters. Weaver and Lord and all of them kept kicking them round the infield and Collins and Bodie couldn't catch nothing.

194

Callahan ought never to of left me in there when he seen how sore my arm was. Why, I couldn't of threw hard enough to break a pain of glass my arm was so sore.

They sure did run wild on the bases. Cobb stole four and Bush and Crawford and Veach about two apiece. Schalk didn't even make a peg half the time. I guess he was trying to throw me down.

The score was sixteen to two when Callahan finally took me out in the eighth and I don't know how many more they got. I kept telling him to take me out when I seen how bad I was but he wouldn't do it. They started bunting in the fifth and Lord and Chase just stood there and didn't give me no help at all.

I was all OK till I had the first two men out in the first inning. Then Crawford come up. I wanted to give him a spitter but Schalk signs me for the fast one and I give it to him. The ball didn't hop much and Crawford happened to catch it just right. At that Collins ought to of catched the ball. Crawford made three bases and up come Cobb. It was the first time I ever seen him. He hollered at me right off the reel. He says You better walk me you busher. I says I will walk you back to the bench. Schalk signs for a spitter and I gives it to him and Cobb misses it.

Then instead of signing for another one Schalk asks for a fast one and I shook my head no but he signed for it again and yells Put something on it. So I throwed a fast one and Cobb hits it right over second base. I don't know what Weaver was doing but he never made a move for the ball. Crawford scored and Cobb was on first base. First thing I knowed he had stole second while I held the ball. Callahan yells Wake up out there and I says Why don't your catcher tell me when they are going to steal. Schalk says Get in there and pitch and shut your mouth. Then I got mad and walked Veach and Moriarity but before I walked Moriarty Cobb and Veach pulled a double steal on Schalk. Gainor lifts a fly and Lord drops it and two more come in. Then Stanage walks and I whiffs their pitcher.

I come in to the bench and Callahan says Are your friends from Bedford up here? I was pretty sore and I says Why don't you get a catcher? He says We don't need no catcher when

195

you're pitching because you can't get nothing past their bats. Then he says You better leave your uniform in here when you go out next inning or Cobb will steal it off your back. I says My arm is sore. He says Use your other one and you'll do just as good.

Gleason says Who do you want to warm up? Callahan says Nobody. He says Cobb is going to lead the league in batting and basestealing anyway so we might as well give him a good start. I was mad enough to punch his jaw but the boys winked at me not to do nothing.

Well I got some support in the next inning and nobody got on. Between innings I says Well I guess I look better now don't I? Callahan says Yes but you wouldn't look so good if Collins hadn't jumped up on the fence and catched that one off Crawford. That's all the encouragement I got Al.

Cobb come up again to start the third and when Schalk signs me for a fast one I shakes my head. Then Schalk says All right pitch anything you want to. I pitched a spitter and Cobb bunts it right at me. I would of threw him out a block but I stubbed my toe in a rough place and fell down. This is the roughest ground I ever seen Al. Veach bunts and for a wonder Lord throws him out. Cobb goes to second and honest Al I forgot all about him being there and first thing I knowed he had stole third. Then Moriarity hits a fly ball to Bodie and Cobb scores though Bodie ought to of threw him out twenty feet.

They batted all round in the fourth inning and scored four or five more. Crawford got the luckiest three-base hit I ever see. He popped one way up in the air and the wind blowed it against the fence. The wind is something fierce here Al. At that Collins ought to of got under it.

I was looking at the bench all the time expecting Callahan to call me in but he kept hollering Go on and pitch. Your friends wants to see you pitch.

Well Al I don't know how they got the rest of their runs but they had more luck than any team I ever seen. And all the time Jennings was on the coaching line yelling like a Indian. Some day Al I'm going to punch his jaw.

After Veach had hit one in the eight Callahan calls me to the bench and says You're through for the day. I says It's about time you found out my arm was sore. He says I ain't worrying about your arm but I'm afraid some of our outfielders will run their legs off and some of them poor infielders will get killed. He says The reporters just sent me a message saying they had run out of paper. Then he says I wish some of the other clubs had pitchers like you so we could hit once in a while. He says Go in the clubhouse and get your arm rubbed off. That's the only way I can get Jennings sore he says.

Well Al that's about all there was to it. It will take two or three stamps to send this but I want you to know the truth about it. The way my arm was I ought never to of went in there.

Yours truly, JACK.

Chicago, Illinois, April 25.
FRIEND AL: Just a line to let you know I am still on earth. My arm feels pretty good again and I guess maybe I will work in Detroit. Violet writes that she can't hardly wait to see me. Looks like I got a regular girl now Al. We go up there the twenty-ninth and maybe I won't be glad to see her. I hope she will be out to the game the day I pitch. I will pitch the way I want to next time and them Tigers won't have such a picnic.

I suppose you seen what the Chicago reporters said about that game. I will punch a couple of their jaws when I see them.

Your pal, JACK.

Chicago, Illinois, April 29.
DEAR OLD AL: Well Al it's over. The club went to Detroit last night and I didn't go along. Callahan told me to report to Comiskey this morning and I went up to the office at ten o'clock. He give me my pay to date and broke the news. I am sold to Frisco.

I asked him how they got waivers on me and he says Oh there was no trouble about that because they all heard how you tamed the Tigers. Then he patted me on the back and says Go out there and work hard boy and maybe you'll get another chance some day. I was kind of choked up so I walked out of the office.

I ain't had no fair deal Al and I ain't going to no Frisco. I will quit the game first and take that job Charley offered me at the billiard hall.

I expect to be in Bedford in a couple of days. I have got to pack up first and settle with my landlady about my room here which I engaged for all season thinking I would be treated square. I am going to rest and lay round home a while and try to forget this rotten game. Tell the boys about it Al and tell them I never would of got let out if I hadn't worked with a sore arm.

I feel sorry for that little girl up in Detroit Al. She expected me there today.

Your old pal, JACK

P.S. I suppose you seen where that lucky lefthander Allen shut out Cleveland with two hits yesterday. The lucky stiff.

San Francisco, California, May 13.

FRIEND AL: I suppose you and the rest of the boys in Bedford will be surprised to learn that I am out here, because I remember telling you when I was sold to San Francisco by the White Sox that not under no circumstances would I report here. I was pretty mad when Comiskey give me my release, because I didn't think I had been given a fair show by Callahan. I don't think so yet Al and I never will but Bill Sullivan the old White Sox catcher talked to me and told me not to pull no boner by refuseing to go where they sent me. He says You're only hurting yourself. He says You must remember that this was your first time up in the big show and very few men no matter how much stuff they got can expect to make good right off the reel. He says All you need is experience and pitching out in the Coast League will be just the thing for you.

So I went in and asked Comiskey for my transportation and he says That's right Boy go out there and work hard and maybe I will want you back. I told him I hoped so but I don't hope nothing of the kind Al. I am going to see if I can't get Detroit to buy me, because I would rather live in Detroit than anywheres else. The little girl who got stuck on me this spring lives there. I guess I told you about her Al. Her name is Violet and she is some

199

queen. And then if I got with the Tigers I wouldn't never have to pitch against Cobb and Crawford, though I believe I could show both of them up if I was right. They ain't got much of a ball club here and hardly any good pitchers outside of me. But I don't care.

I will win some games if they give me any support and I will get back in the big league and show them birds something. You know me, Al.

Your pal, JACK.

CONTACT

MALORIE BLACKMAN

ARL'S COMPUTER STARTED BEEPING. Someone was phoning him. Wondering if he'd ever finish his homework, Carl ordered his computer, "Answer call."

Instantly the geological map of Neptune that he'd been studying disappeared, to be replaced by Gina's face.

"Carl, I've got some bad news." For once Gina wasn't smiling.

"Hello to you too! What's the matter?"

"It's about our football match tomorrow."

"What about it?" Carl was instantly wary.

"Graeme's been asking questions," Gina said grimly.

"Oh no!" Carl's heart sank.

Gina shook her head, a bitter frown on her lips. Carl knew she despised her twin brother more than he or any of her other friends did. Graeme was renowned for never thinking of, or caring about, anyone but himself. He set a new standard for being totally and utterly selfish.

"I told him that it's only a five-a-side and that we already have ten players but he's insisting that we let him sit in as a reserve."

"And what did you say?"

"I told him that he couldn't, of course," Gina replied indignantly. "But you know what Graeme's like. That's not going to stop him. So I thought I'd better phone everyone in the game to warn them."

"How did he find out about our game in the first place?" Carl fumed.

"Hey! Don't bite my head off. I didn't tell him," Gina snapped back.

Carl took a deep breath, then another, in an effort to calm down. Graeme knew about their game . . . Playing football the way they played it was dangerous enough, without having to worry about Graeme finding out about it as well.

"What's Graeme doing now?"

"Phoning around, trying to find out who else is playing," said Gina. "I think he's hoping someone will say yes to him sitting in as the reserve."

"Did he ask *where* we're playing?" asked Carl.

"Yeah, but I told him not to be so nosy. I said if he wasn't playing then he didn't need to know," Gina replied.

"That won't stop him."

"I know."

Carl clenched his fists inside his NC suit. How on earth had Graeme found out about the football match? It didn't make any sense. None of the team would've told him, Carl was sure of that. They all had too much to lose if anyone outside the team found out what was really going on.

Gina turned away from the screen to listen to something out of Carl's earshot, before turning back. "I've got to go. Dad's calling me. I'll see you tomorrow."

"Maybe we ought to cancel tomorrow's match – just to be on the safe side?" said Carl thoughtfully.

"No way! You can't do that," Gina said immediately. "We only get to play once a month as it is and I've been looking forward to our game since the day after the last one!"

"It'd be better to postpone the game tomorrow than risk being found out – and worse, not playing ever again," Carl pointed out.

Gina pursed her lips. "I suppose so," she agreed reluctantly. "Look, phone me tomorrow morning and let me know what's happening."

"Disconnect call," Carl ordered his computer.

The geological map of Neptune reappeared. Carl's mum popped her head around his bedroom door.

"Hi Carl. Your dinner's ready."

"Mum . . ." Carl swivelled around in his chair. "Mum, what would happen if I took off my NC suit?"

"Take off your Non-Contact suit?" Carl's mum was horrified. She straightened up and came into the room. "You wouldn't do such a thing, would you?"

"No. I just wondered what would happen if I did?" Carl shook his head quickly.

"You'd die," Carl's mum said without hesitation. "Without the Non-Contact suits, we'd all die. They protect us from pollution and fallout and more importantly, diseases."

"Yes, but . . ."

"No 'buts'. Contact with another person would be lethal," Mum said sternly.

Slowly, Carl turned back to his computer.

"Carl, dear, don't you think I'd love to give you a hug – a proper hug – without the Non-Contact suits separating us? Don't you think I'd love to hold my own son? But it's too dangerous. We humans almost got wiped off the planet two hundred years ago, thanks to the contact we had with other people. Believe me, this is much safer."

"I guess so," said Carl. "I just wonder sometimes what it'd be like to touch someone's arm. Or what other people smell like. Or what it'd be like to see someone smile without an NC mask over their face."

"What's brought this on all of sudden?" Mum frowned.

"Nothing in particular," Carl replied quickly. He was getting on to dangerous ground. He shouldn't have said anything. Mum was no fool and she might suspect something if he kept asking more questions. "I'll have my dinner now."

Carl walked over to the nutrition unit in his room and plugged the feed tube of his NC suit into it. He watched, preoccupied, as his pureed dinner was delivered along the tube and straight into his stomach. The tube in his stomach could only be activated and opened by a proper feed tube so it was perfectly safe. Once again, Carl found himself vaguely wondering what it would be like to chew and taste real, solid food. Actually having to *chew* your food was such a weird idea, but isn't that what they'd had to do over two hundred years ago? So many things had changed . . . Carl's thoughts turned back to the match.

What was Graeme doing now? he wondered. Trying to find out more about the football game, no doubt.

And if he *did* find out . . .?

Carl shook his head. They'd all just have to make sure that he didn't. There'd be hell to pay otherwise.

Carl frowned suddenly. Something wasn't right. With a start, he turned his head. His mum was watching him silently. Neither of them said a word.

"Carl, be careful – OK?" Mum said at last.

Before Carl could answer, she left the room.

The following morning, whilst Carl and his family were plugged into the nutrition unit for their breakfast, Graeme phoned. Carl went into his bedroom to take the call, much to his mum and dad's amusement. Carl switched his computer to videophone mode. He guessed what Graeme was phoning about – and he wasn't wrong.

"Hi Carl." Graeme's smile was bright and false. "How're you?"

"Fine."

"I . . . er . . . I hear you, Gina and some others are playing football this afternoon?"

Graeme was momentarily thrown by Carl's monosyllabic answer. "So?"

"Gina said I have to ask you. Can I play too?"

"No. Sorry. We have all the people we need," Carl replied crisply, annoyed at Gina for passing the buck to him.

"But I could act as reserve in case someone can't make it or has to leave the game before it's over. Please . . ."

"No."

"At least tell me where you're playing so I can set up my PC to watch," said Graeme.

"No. It's a private game."

"Why can't I at least watch? It's just a virtual football game, for goodness' sake. Why all the secrecy?" Graeme asked with suspicion.

"It's no secret. We just don't want you watching, that's all." Carl shrugged.

"Then I'll key in to every playing field in this area until I find you," Graeme threatened. "I have a virtual play helmet too. You can't stop me from finding you and watching."

And with that Graeme hung up. Carl sighed and leaned back in his chair. He hadn't handled that very well at all, but Graeme got on his nerves. Carl turned to look at his virtual play helmet which was hanging on the NC suit stand in the corner of his room. He eyed it with distaste. After each monthly football game, the helmet grew more and more loathsome to him.

Over seventy years ago, scientists had come up with a way in which team games could be played without any contact whatsoever being made with any other person – the virtual helmets. In the privacy of your own room, you connected up the virtual play helmet to your Non-Contact suit and plugged it into your computer. Everyone else who was playing in the team game – be it football, basketball, rounders or whatever – did the same. Then you specified where you were going to play, who was in your team and who was on the opposing side. Each person's computer would then link up and the computers would do the rest. You then played a game of virtual reality football. Even though each player was in their own room, totally alone, it didn't look like that. It looked as if you were really on the field with everyone else – wearing the virtual suits but still together. It was a brilliant way of ensuring that there was no real contact between the players. Oh, you could kick the ball and the NC suit made it feel and look like you were kicking it. But you weren't really. It was all a computer game, and it wasn't *real*. Even so, you weren't allowed to tackle. Tackling, or rather *trying* to tackle, was a sending-off offence. Carl thought that was one of the most stupid rules. Instead of tackling, you could only run so far with the ball before you had to pass, or the ball went to the other side – those were the rules.

Carl sighed. He preferred the way he and his friends played. He couldn't go back to playing football the virtual way, he just couldn't.

Later that morning, Carl phoned Gina.

"Are you alone?" he asked.

Gina nodded. "Are we still on for this afternoon?"

"Has your brother given up yet?"

"What d'you think?" Gina snorted with derision.

Carl thought for a long moment. Should he postpone the game or not? No, he wouldn't. He *couldn't*.

"We'll play, but we'll be very careful," he said. "Gina, you've got to be especially careful."

"Understood." Gina nodded. And with that, she disconnected the call.

After lunch, Carl made his way to a secluded part of the derelict wasteland outside the city gates. He asked himself over and over if he was doing the right thing.

He didn't have the answer.

Carl was the last to arrive. Everyone else was there before him. He looked around. Graeme wasn't there. Carl could feel every tense muscle in his body begin to relax.

"We thought you weren't going to show up," said Gina.

"As if!" Carl grinned.

"Is it safe?" Andrew asked anxiously.

"Course it is," said Carl.

And he began to unzip his Non-Contact suit. The others looked around before they did the same.

They always waited for Carl to take off his NC suit first. After all, he and Andrew had been the first ones to play football without their suits. Then Tariq, Gina and slowly over many months their numbers had grown to ten true and trusted friends. Carl kicked off his NC suit to stand in his shorts, NC boots and a T-shirt, as did the others. Carl took a deep breath and raised his hands to the sky. The air dancing over his skin felt like the whisper of heaven. A slight breeze blew. It was amazing but a year ago, Carl hadn't even known about a little but wondrous thing like a gentle breeze and how good it could feel whispering across his face.

Carl and the others stood in a circle, hand in hand. Once again Carl marvelled at the feel of real fingers. Not virtual fingers or fingers enlosed in an NC glove but real live fingers! Clammy, moist, warm, soft fingers! Even the most sophisticated NC suit couldn't match that.

"Ready?" Carl asked everyone.

They all nodded.

"All for one and one for all and no one must know!" They all chanted solemnly. "Let's play!"

Tariq threw out the ball – a makeshift sphere made out of synothnyl packed with soft wadding – and the game began.

Real tackling. *Contact!* Real elbowing. *Contact!* And when Andrew scored a goal, everyone around him, even those on the opposing side gathered round him to pat him on the back or hug him or lift him into the air.

Carl beamed at everyone as they ran up and down the wasteland pitch. It was like being truly human for one afternoon a month. Only on this pitch did he feel alive. The virtual pitch just couldn't compare. The outcome didn't matter. The score didn't matter. The game did. They weren't robots or bits and bytes in a computer any more – they were real kids! Carl was sure flying and swooping and soaring couldn't be any better.

But something was wrong. One by one the players on the pitch froze and stared past him.

"So this is where you've all got to, is it?"

Carl's head snapped round with dismay.

It was Graeme.

No one spoke. No one moved. They all stared horror-stricken. Graeme looked around with narrowed eyes. He then turned to Carl, eyeing Carl's shorts and boots and his T-shirt which was damp with perspiration.

"Graeme, you followed me. You toad! You shouldn't have . . ."

"No, Gina. Don't," Carl interrupted her.

"I told you I'd find you," Graeme said at last.

Silence.

"Physical contact of any kind isn't allowed," Graeme continued. He tilted his head to one side, puzzled. "Aren't you all afraid you're going to breathe in something deadly or catch something and die?"

"Well, it hasn't happened yet," said Carl. "And what's more, playing football this way is *fun*, like nothing else on Earth. D'you want to try it?"

"You're only asking me to join you to stop me from telling the authorities what you're all up to," said Graeme.

"That's part of it – true," Carl admitted. "But you know about us now. Whether you tell or not is your decision, but don't go without at least trying it."

"But it's dangerous." Graeme sounded unsure.

"No, it isn't." Gina stepped forward. "We're all still alive. Just try it."

Graeme looked around again. Every eye was upon him.

"Even if I did play, I'd still tell what you're all up to," Graeme said firmly.

Gina opened her mouth to argue but Carl got in first.

"That's up to you," he said with a calm he was far from feeling. "But you can't leave now, otherwise you'll always wonder what it would've been like. This is your chance to find out."

Everyone else moved up slowly to stand around Carl, facing Graeme. No one made any sudden movements. It was if they didn't want to scare Graeme away.

Cautiously, Graeme unfastened his gloves first and took them off. He stared down at his bare hands and clenched them suddenly. As he looked up, Carl smiled. Graeme's hands relaxed. He unzipped his NC suit and stepped out of it to stand in shorts and a T-shirt like everyone else.

"D'you want me to help you take off your helmet?" Carl volunteered.

"No, I'll do it myself." Graeme's voice was low and nervous.

With trembling fingers, he unfastened the straps at the sides of his helmet. He pulled it off his head with a gasp.

"You can be on my side. OK?" Carl held out his hand.

Graeme looked down at it – anxiety and suspicion spreading over his face in equal measure. Carl thrust his hand further forward.

"My teeth are in my mouth, not my hand! It won't bite you," Carl smiled.

Slowly, Graeme took hold of his hand. Carl recognized the shock and wonder on Graeme's face, because it had been on his face too the first time he played football without his NC suit. What had started off as a silly dare between two friends had grown into something strangely addictive. Carl's smile widened as Graeme looked at him with bewildered astonishment.

"Welcome to our game!" Carl grinned, having to use considerable force to pull his hand away. He turned to the others around him. "OK team, Graeme's on our side. Let's give him hell!"

The next forty-five minutes produced one of the best times Carl had ever had – as well as producing some of the best football any of them had ever played. Players from both sides used any excuse to let Graeme have it! He was bumped into, tackled – more often to the ground, than not – brought down, hacked, elbowed and even head-butted once in the stomach by his sister, Gina.

And he loved it!

He wasn't a bad football player either. And after he'd begun to get used to actually running up and down the pitch beyond the confines of a computer simulation, it was as if he'd been a member of the group forever. He certainly gave as good as he got, relishing each knock he had with the others. But all too soon, Carl had to call a halt. "Our time's up, guys," he said reluctantly.

"Could we play for just a little longer?" Andrew protested with everyone else agreeing.

Carl shook his head. "You all know how it works. We're all meant to be round at someone else's house playing virtual football. If we're late home our parents will start phoning around. We've got away with it so far – we don't want to blow it now."

Grumbling, as they did every month, the whole group formed a circle and held hands. Graeme stood watching, not sure what was going on.

"Come on, Graeme – you too," Carl beckoned to him.

Graeme walked over to stand between Gina and Carl. He took hold of their hands, part of the circle.

"D'you know something?" Gina smiled at her brother. "You're not too bad!"

"That's the first time I can remember you smiling at me," Graeme told her softly.

"Are you still going to tell on us?" The moment Carl asked the question, the mood of the group changed. The circle was broken as hands were dropped to their sides. Some looked down at their feet, some looked away towards the city walls, a few looked at Carl. No one looked at Graeme.

"What d'you think?" Graeme said at last.

"Graeme . . ." Gina didn't get any further.

She wasn't the only one who was disappointed – to say the least. Carl felt his whole body slump with misery.

"How could I pulverize all of you the next time, if I told anyone about our game?" said Graeme. And he started laughing. Moments later, everyone was doing the same – albeit nervously for the most part.

"You should've seen your faces," Graeme grinned, but then his smile faded. "I *was* going to tell – before I took my NC suit off, but it's different now. It's as if we're all *connected* somehow."

"Welcome to our group," said Carl. "We have an oath we say before and after each game and if you're going to be part of us, you must say it too – but before that, BUNDLE! Get him everyone for winding us up!"

And half of them piled on top of Graeme before the other half lifted him high on to their shoulders.

"He doesn't even look like my brother any more," Gina whispered happily to Carl. "He looks different somehow."

"Yeah. For the first time he looks real, part of something like the rest of us," said Carl. "I think we've reached him. I think we've made contact."

ON TOP OF THE WORLD

ALAN DURANT

A BLARE OF TRUMPETS followed by a huge roar greeted the medal winners as they entered the stadium. Heading the medal entourage just as he had his fellow competitors in the final, Matt raised an arm aloft to acknowledge the crowd, his face a picture of delight. He could never, he knew, feel any better than this. No one could. This was as good as life got, winning a gold medal at the Olympic Games, the most celebrated and long-contested sporting event in the history of the world. This was what every athlete dreamed of and strove for, and so few achieved. And he was one of those few.

His legs felt as light now as they'd felt heavy when he'd stumbled out of the arena after his lap of honour, exhausted but triumphant, barely an hour ago. Striding across cinder, then grass on his way to the presentation rostrum, he was walking on cloud. All around people were waving flags and applauding – and most of all, they were applauding him, Matt Douglas, the new Olympic 10,000 metres champion. Happiness surged in him, bringing him close to tears.

As he reached the rostrum, he turned and waved to his parents and to his coach, Tom, who raised both thumbs in the air in a joyous salute. Matt's grin grew even broader as he returned the gesture. He knew how much his winning meant to Tom – and what a huge part he'd played in helping him to achieve it. Matt would never have got to where he was now without the great patience and expertise of his coach. The gold medal was as much Tom's as his own, Matt considered.

On the other side of the stadium, the pole vault was in progress and the medal presentation was delayed briefly. Matt didn't care; he was in no hurry. He wanted these moments to last forever. He'd watched this part of the Games on the TV often enough and now he was actually here he wanted to savour everything. He got goosepimples suddenly, thinking of all those millions of people around the world whose eyes would be on him now, anticipating his step up on to the winner's podium and the celebrations that would follow.

While he waited, Matt's gaze dropped to trackside. It fixed on a boy, about eleven Matt guessed, near the front of the crowd, sitting high on someone's shoulders – his dad's probably – small flag in hand, waving wildly. Matt smiled, his mind slipping back to a time when *he* was a boy, eleven years old . . . In that instant, he was no longer in the enormous purpose-built Olympic stadium on a warm summer's evening; he was in a suburban park on a chilly mid autumn afternoon, the day of the Inter Schools Cross Country Championship, the day it had all begun.

They'd been preparing for months. Every Saturday morning they'd come down to the park for a training run. Matt would rather have been out with his mates playing football, but there was no choice involved. The Inter Schools Cross Country was the biggest event on Mornington School's sporting calendar and if you were picked, you ran; Mr Brookes, the head teacher, insisted on it. Matt enjoyed the running OK but he didn't like the fact that he *had* to do it – and he wasn't too keen on those cold autumn mornings either. The boys went for a jog to warm up before they raced but they never seemed to get really warm. Matt hated that moment when he had to strip off his tracksuit, feeling the cold air against his skin, and take his place on the starting line. There were twelve in the squad, though only eight would take part in the actual competition. In training, Matt generally finished third or fourth – though Mr Brookes said he ought to do better. He was right too, Matt knew it, but somehow he couldn't do anything about it. He lacked confidence and belief in himself. Part of the problem was nerves. Before every race, Matt felt terrible. Butterflies did fluttery somersaults in his stomach, his legs felt rubbery, he wanted to go to the toilet, though he'd only just been. When the race got underway, he was always at the back, and by the time he'd recovered, he was far behind the front runners – too far behind to catch them, he believed. He'd improve his position steadily through the race and put in a terrific sprint finish to end up well-placed, but he could never catch up with the winners. A top twenty finish in the Inter Schools was the best he could hope for, it seemed.

The competition took place in the park in which Mornington trained, so they had the advantage of home terrain. The weather was damp and chilly. It had rained the day before and the ground was muddy, the grass strewn with brown, sodden leaves. Fifteen schools in all were to take part, with Mornington and their traditional rivals John Fisher the favourites. Every runner's position counted in the overall result and, after Assembly on the morning of the race, Mr Brookes emphasized to his team the importance of finishing as high as possible. This was the moment for each of them to run his best race ever, he said, and it appeared to Matt that, as he spoke these words, the head teacher was looking directly at him.

Arriving at the park, Matt was struck immediately by the buzz around the place. The atmosphere was about as different as it could be from those Saturday morning training runs. There were people everywhere: teachers, parents, competitors . . . No longer was this a sleepy suburban park; now it was an intense and noisy sporting arena. The effect it had on Matt was dramatic. The nervousness that usually affected him so badly was submerged beneath a tide of excitement. As he lined up for the start, the butterflies still fluttered in his stomach, he still felt as if he needed to go to the toilet, but there was no rubberiness to his legs – they felt fresh and strong. Standing in the midst of this great throng of runners, each of them wearing a vest in his school's colours, Matt felt a thrill he'd never known before. For the first time in his life, he felt like a runner, as if this was where he belonged.

He didn't get the best of starts, despite his lack of nerves. It was difficult getting away well in that huge company and, besides, old habits die hard. By the time he reached the stone bridge at four hundred metres there were fifty or more runners ahead of him. For the next fifteen hundred metres, he caught up and passed competitors at a steady rate. This race was following the usual pattern. And yet, what he felt inside was by no means usual. He felt full of power and adrenalin. There was a rhythm to his running that had never been there before – except sometimes when he'd run in the dark and his feet seemed to fly. The ground was heavy but he felt light and totally at ease. When he reached the bend in the course that was the halfway marker, he increased his pace, passing runners at will.

By the time the entry to the woods came in sight, there were only a dozen or so runners in front of him, the leader about two hundred metres ahead. A large crowd had gathered at the edge of the wood, urging on their favourites. As Matt approached he saw his own parents there, shouting along with the rest. He'd never seen them so animated and it gave him a real lift. As he passed them, vanishing into the trees, he accelerated, flying by a competitor in a John Fisher vest. At this point in a race he usually took things easy, believing himself beaten and saving his energy for the final two-hundred-metre sprint; but not today. Today, he believed anything was possible. Today, he was going to run the race of his life. Already he was doing better than he'd ever done before – only two of his own team members were ahead of him, along with a couple from John Fisher and one or two from other schools.

His breathing was good, his stride smooth and rhythmic. The ground in the woods was firmer and encouraged him to increase his pace. He pounded by another runner and another, in a heady blur of golden trees . . . Now only Mornington's cross county

champion and captain, Chris Downes, was in front of him, battling for the lead with two John Fisher boys. The distance between Matt and the leaders was still around a hundred metres and less than eight hundred metres of the race remained. Already he'd far exceeded expectations. Should he be happy now with what he'd achieved – settle for fourth place? No one would blame him – quite the contrary, everyone would be delighted with his performance. But why stop now? He was tiring a little but still feeling OK. Any thoughts of resting on his laurels were dispelled by the yelling of the spectators up ahead. They must have seen the first glimpses of the leading group, he concluded, approaching the woods' exit.

He raced on, gaining all the time on the small group in front, one of whom – one of the two John Fisher runners – was losing ground rapidly. So rapidly he almost seemed to be going backwards, Matt thought as he caught and passed him. Coming out of the woods, he was forty metres down with three hundred to go. The finishing line was round a corner, out of sight, but he could hear the excited babble as the crowd prepared to greet the leaders. He was sprinting now, but without his usual fluency. He'd pushed himself harder than ever and discovered, to his consternation, that there was little left in the tank. He wasn't going to zip over the final strait the way he normally did. It was all about guts and willpower now. He thrust himself on, his breathing ragged and hoarse.

A hundred and fifty metres from the finish he overtook an exhausted Chris Dawes, who'd fallen back from the leader. The tape was in sight and the crowd's shouting grew frenzied as they saw Matt advancing – and the possibility of a close finish. The John Fisher boy responded with a new surge, but it quickly faded. He had nothing left, Matt quickly realized, and it gave him renewed heart. He summoned every last gram of strength in his legs to drag himself forward.

"Sprint!" he exhorted himself. "Sprint!"

A hundred metres, ninety, eighty, seventy, sixty . . . Fifty metres to go and he was just a pace behind, but hurting – boy, was he hurting! Forty metres, thirty, twenty . . . Going into the roped-off area that marked the final ten metres, the two boys were side by side, struggling, striving, almost stumbling, everything a haze of noise and colour. Matt kicked again. His head was roaring, his chest exploding as he crossed the line and fell, fell, into his dad's arms.

When he looked up feebly, panting uncontrollably, the exultant smile on his dad's face – and on the face of Mr Brookes behind him – said it all. He'd won! For the first time in his life – and against all odds – he'd won! Matt was the Inter Schools Cross Country Champion and Mornington, surely, would win the team trophy now. He could barely summon the energy to smile, but inside he was jubilant. This was a day he knew he'd remember always.

". . . the Olympic Gold Medallist at 10,000 metres, Matthew Douglas!" The announcement jolted Matt out of his reverie. Suddenly, he was back in the present, stepping up on to the podium to accept the greatest accolade any athlete could win: an Olympic gold medal. The crowds shouted their approval as the ribbon was placed over his head by the President of the Olympic Games, and they shook hands. Then Matt was presented with a bouquet of flowers and he shook hands once more. His head was in a whirl as he stood up straight and looked down at the solid metal medal that hung heavily around his neck. He lifted it up to see the Olympian figure embossed on its face, then, almost as if to prove to himself that it was real and to the delight of the photographers and the crowd, he kissed it.

There was a genuine spirit of camaraderie and sportsmanship on the rostrum. When the other successful athletes were presented with their medals, all three shook hands and embraced. They'd competed against each other often in the past and they knew each other well. This had been the closest race they'd ever contested – only two metres separating them – and the closeness of the struggle was reflected in the warmth of the reception afforded them by the spectators, none warmer than that of the boy sitting astride his dad's shoulders, waving and yelling. Matt wondered momentarily if one day that boy might also become a champion. As the first strains of the national anthem resounded round the stadium, Matt could no longer hold back the tears.

It had been a long haul from the Inter Schools Cross Country Championship to victory in the Olympic Games. A long, hard, haul. But it had been worth it. Boy, it had been worth it! Standing there on the winner's rostrum, Matt Douglas was on top of the world.

ACKNOWLEDGEMENTS

The publisher would like to thank the copyright holders for permission to reproduce the following copyright material:

Enid Bagnold: Extract from *National Velvet* by Enid Bagnold. Copyright © The Estate of Enid Bagnold 1935. First published by William Heinemann Ltd and used with permission of Egmont Children's Books Limited, London. **Malorie Blackman:** "Contact" by Malorie Blackman from *Out of this World* chosen by Wendy Cooling. Copyright © Malorie Blackman 1997. Used by permission of Orion Children's Books. **John Branfield:** "Wet Bob, Dry Bob" by John Branfield from *A Sporting Chance: Stories of Winning and Losing* compiled by Aidan Chambers. Copyright © John Branfield 1985. Used by permission of A. P. Watt Ltd on behalf of John Branfield. **Matt Christopher:** Extract from *Wingman On Ice* by Matt Christopher. Copyright © 1964 by Catherine M. Christopher; copyright © 1992 by Catherine M. Christopher. Used by permission of Little, Brown and Company (Inc.). **Tessa Duder:** Extract from *Alex* by Tessa Duder. Copyright © Tessa Duder 1987. Used by permission of Oxford University Press. **Thomas J. Dygard:** "Just Once" by Thomas J. Dygard, from *Ultimate Sports* by Donald R. Gallo. Copyright © 1995 by Donald R. Gallo. Used by permission of Random House Children's Books, a division of Random House, Inc. **Michael Hardcastle:** "Talk Us Through It" from *Dog Bites Goalie* by Michael Hardcastle. Copyright © Michael Hardcastle 1993. First published by Methuen Children's Books, an imprint of Egmont Children's Books Limited, London and used with permission. **Ring Lardner:** Extract from *You Know Me Al* by Ring Lardner. Copyright © 1925 by Charles Scribner's Sons, renewed by Ellis A. Lardner. Reprinted with the permission of Scribner, a division of Simon & Schuster. **Judith Logan Lehne:** "The Blue Darter" by Judith Logan Lehne from *The Blue Darter and Other*

Sports Stories. Copyright © 1992 by Highlights for Children, Inc., Columbus, Ohio. **Julius Lester:** Extract from *Basketball Game* by Julius Lester. Copyright © Julius Lester 1972. Used by permission of Laura Cecil Literary Agency. **Jan Mark:** "Feet" from *Feet and Other Stories* by Jan Mark. Copyright © Jan Mark 1980. Used by permission of David Higham Associates. **Walter Dean Myers:** Extract from *Slam!* by Walter Dean Myers. Published by Scholastic Press a division of Scholastic Inc. Copyright © 1996 by Walter Dean Myers. Reprinted by permission. **Bill Naughton:** "Spit Nolan" from *The Goalkeeper's Revenge* by Bill Naughton. Copyright © Bill Naughton 1961. Used by permission of Thomas Nelson and Sons Ltd. **Philippa Pearce:** "The Running-Companion" from *The Shadow-Cage and Other Tales of the Supernatural* by Philippa Pearce (Kestrel, 1977). Copyright © Philippa Pearce 1977. Reproduced by permission of Penguin Books Ltd. **Tom Tully:** "Goal of the Day" from *Roy of the Rovers: Come On You Reds!* by Tom Tully. Copyright © Egmont Fleetway Ltd. Used by permission of Egmont Fleetway Limited. **Will Weaver:** "Stealing for Girls" by Will Weaver, from *Ultimate Sports* by Donald R. Gallo. Copyright © 1995 by Donald R. Gallo. Used by permission of Random House Children's Books, a division of Random House, Inc. **Jacqueline Wilson:** Extract from *Cliffhanger* by Jacqueline Wilson. Copyright © Jacqueline Wilson 1995. Published by Corgi Yearling, a division of Transworld Publishers. All rights reserved. **P. G. Wodehouse:** Extract from *Mike at Wrykyn* by P. G. Wodehouse. Used by permission of A. P. Watt Ltd on behalf of The Trustees of the Wodehouse Estate.

Titles in the Story Library Series